FIRST BORN

Love & Dark Series

Book 2

HINA MCCORD & BECCA C. SMITH

Published by Red Frog Publishing, a division of Red Frog
Media

Visit our website at www.2nerdgirls.com

First published in 2015

The characters and events portrayed in this book are fictitious.
Any similarity to real persons, living or dead, is coincidental
and not intended by the author.

ISBN 9781949877267

Printed in the United States of America

To all the nerds out there. Never give up, never surrender!

PROLOGUE
CAELIUS

The sound of his sobbing filled my heart with more warmth than my first day under Egypt's sun. No amount of light could penetrate me the way his cries did now. And I'd waited. So many years ago I'd longed to see his flesh torn apart.

It was bittersweet. I smiled, licking blood from my arm as I dropped another one of his lifeless children. I could make this so much sweeter. My patience had worn thin over the centuries, but what were a few more days to relish in his agony? This kind of theatrics needed an audience, and the spectator I had in mind would be moved beyond reason with this display.

I laced my hand through the curls of his golden hair. His blue eyes were wet as his lips trembled. "Oh come, Gracuri," I said. "You can do better. These are the children you first turned that I'm feasting on; surely you can beg louder than this. Just call Lucian's name, and I'll spare them."

He was weak. In the last few days he'd submitted himself

to my every whim, every bodily pleasure and destruction, all to save his children, but I was just carrying out a sentence I'd given Lucian. I was finishing the cleansing of his line.

I decapitated Gracuri's *favorite* child. His body sagged. I leaned my head close to his slumped frame. If he wasn't dead, if my Lucian hadn't given him the blessing of an immortal kiss, this would have killed him.

I listened as his heart seized in his chest. His body twitched and convulsed: a heart attack. The fresh human blood I'd force-fed through his veins kept him alive. I wanted him awake and fully charged for today's tortures.

"I'm so sorry. Did you *love* him? You know, the *first* one we turn is always our most dear. The pain of love lost, well, it's driven immortals and gods greater than yourself to madness."

I smiled, leaning on his back. It was like resting on a bed of stones. Lucian was more comfortable. I glanced up at the night sky, thinking of my son. It was beautiful, all that black emptiness. I growled and, for a moment, Gracuri's agony left me hollow. All those stars were ruining the darkness with their light; all that noise was polluting the silence.

I missed it, the power. The feeling of twisting into a black hole and devouring galaxies was thrilling. But when the Light became obsessed with these small worlds, with mammals and in particular humans, well, I was curious enough to make a bargain.

This small form was nothing compared to my true essence. It wasn't even a fraction, yet I clung to it desperately. That was the agreement: I could take *this* form *once*. And it was worth it. All of that power as Darkness seemed meaningless once I was solid. Before my essence was scattered, but now I could think clearly. I was free from the burden of balance.

His convulsing stopped, and I sighed. "You know what the most irritating thing about you is, Gracuri?" I rolled to face him, cupping his chin in my hands as his pupils constricted and his fangs bared.

I looked at the poor thing with unexpected gratitude, whispering into his ear, "You're so pathetic. I've killed you in hundreds of unique ways this week, but my Lucian would take all of this without dying and reviving. Lucian would take it until he was mangled, near death. He wouldn't let himself go. But you, Gracuri, you're not worthy of such a father. Your very existence shames him and, in that way, shames me. Your love makes him *weak*. But *my* love will make him strong."

CHAPTER 1
SHEA

It was impossible to concentrate when Lucian looked at me like that. He was supposed to be teaching me how to use my powers, but his eyes would go all intense, and it made me want to jump the guy.

"Shea, don't look at me like that," Lucian said.

"Me? You're the one with smolder-face. I just really want to make this water move." I'd been trying to connect to a small pond just outside the villa near Paris where we were staying. Lucian had shown me a few tricks for focusing my energy, but my mind tended to veer back to him rather than the dirty pool of water.

He stepped closer, and my heart raced. Talk about having it bad for someone. One gesture, move, look, kiss . . .

I put my hand out before he could touch me, almost touching the necklace he always wore around his neck. "Hold it right there, bud-o. You start with the kissing, and my brain is mush for the rest of the day."

He didn't listen.

As usual.

His arms pulled me close, and my knees almost gave. How could one guy be so freaking hot? It wasn't fair to the rest of us mere mortals when someone like Lucian existed. With his teal eyes and sculpted face, not to mention his perfectly coifed dark hair, he was too perfect.

I wasn't *ugly*. I was cute by most standards—long blond hair, decent body, hazel eyes—but standing next to *him*? It was the difference between a Michelangelo and a hotel painting.

Of course, I was probably biased because I loved Lucian with every fiber of my soul. I hated being insecure, but I still couldn't totally believe he felt the same way for me.

Then I felt his lips against mine.

Yup. Pure mush.

I felt his hunger as he pressed his body against me, his mouth passionately devouring my lips. It was how we spent most of our days. We weren't even married, but our honeymoon phase showed no signs of abating.

Which I had zero problems with.

Before this inevitably led us back to our bedroom, I managed to muster up enough self-restraint to pull away, uttering breathlessly, "We can't. Caelius is still out there. I need to be strong."

At the mention of his father, Lucian nodded and took a step back. "You're right. Your power may be the weapon we need to stop him. His blood pumping through my veins makes me vulnerable to his influence."

That must have been hard for him to admit.

Lucian had tried to explain it, though it was still difficult for me to fully grasp. Apparently, Lucian was the first and only vampire made by Caelius, who in turn was Darkness in human form.

From what Lucian knew, it was Caelius's blood that turned a human into a vampire, which was why Lucian was the strongest. But Caelius's blood diluted from there with each person turned, so the weakest vampire would probably only have a single drop of Caelius's blood in him. It would make him strong, but nowhere near "Lucian strong." Plus, Lucian had said when a vampire *made* another vampire they shared some kind of blood bond with each other as well.

In the simplest terms, the maker's blood was also running through their veins. And, with that kind of connection, makers could control their offspring—to a certain degree. Lucian had explained that resistance against makers depended on how strong the vampire was. The more inner strength a vampire had, the less control the maker had over them.

I knew Lucian was strong even if he didn't. When the time came for the two of us to face Caelius, I trusted Lucian to fight against the blood of his maker like he'd done before when he'd fought Caelius in his prison. If I saw Caelius again, it would be too soon, but fighting him was our destiny.

We had to kill him before he wreaked havoc on the planet. After all, the odds were on our side already: Caelius was still weak from escaping.

I still couldn't believe he'd broken free. I knew it was my fault, but Lucian and Aidan wouldn't let me take the blame, so I kept the self-loathing to myself.

"You'll be able to face him again and be even stronger this time." I tried to sound as encouraging as I could.

Lucian didn't respond, he only nodded, which translated to "I don't want to argue the point." I understood. He wasn't looking forward to a daddy-son reunion outside the cage any more than I was.

Avoiding the issue, Lucian reverted back to instructor mode. "Take a deep breath and focus on the water. I want you to create a whirlpool."

The fact that we were doing this during the day was pretty amazing. When the prison had broken, so had the curse that'd kept vampires from the sun. Lucian couldn't seem to get enough of the stuff. After three thousand years in darkness, I could hardly blame him.

"A whirlpool . . ." Lucian's voice nudged me back to the task at hand.

"Okay." I shook out my hands and jogged in place as if I were a boxer about to enter the ring. "Pond, right. Swirly motion, okay." I clapped my hands together and took in a gulp of fresh air and . . . nothing.

"You're getting frustrated. I can see it in every tense muscle on your beautiful body." Lucian had meant to be encouraging, but hearing him say the word "beautiful" in regard to me made my head spin. Then he added, "You can connect to the earth and trees easily now, but if you could master *all* the elements, you would be a real threat to Caelius."

"Rub it in," I grumbled under my breath. I knew he was trying to give me props for my earth mastery, if I could call it mastery. After Caelius's escape three months ago, Lucian had decided earth was a good place to start, since I'd had some luck with it in the past. Within a few days I'd turned the foliage outside our villa into serious bodyguards. From swiping, to strangling, to punching, I felt like I'd created my own Ents from *Lord of the Rings*. It was kind of awesome.

But mastery over earth was as far as I seemed to be able to go; every other element was like a brick wall to me. Okay, I'd had a little luck with air once when I'd created a tornado to save Aidan from a vamp, but I'd been under extreme stress then. For some reason I couldn't recreate what I'd done.

It had been my idea to try water today. I'd been reading Greek mythology books about Poseidon and had felt inspired. Not that we'd be running into Caelius on a sea voyage, but at this point I wanted to add another element under my belt. Besides, manipulating water, creating tidal waves, and controlling whirlpools just sounded cool.

But right now all I was doing was staring at a mossy, stagnant body of water that I could barely cause a ripple on. And I was pretty sure that ripple had been from the wind, not me.

"I'm trying to get you to relax." Lucian gave me a half smile that never failed to make my face flush.

"Well, relaxing isn't really an option around you." I shook my head. "It's easier when I'm being attacked or I need to protect someone."

"I'm not going to attack you, if that's what you're asking. At least not in a way you wouldn't enjoy."

There was that smile again.

The boy was going to give me a heart attack. He was so damn sexy. And *mine*.

Lucian cocked his head to the side. "Did you just pinch yourself?"

Busted. But I couldn't help it. The good parts of my life felt like an amazing dream I never wanted to wake up from, and the bad parts felt like nightmares I *couldn't* wake up from. "I'm going to concentrate," I announced.

If it wasn't for distraction-boy, I might've had a shot at making this water do *something*. At this point I debated jumping in just to cool off.

I closed my eyes and thought only of the pond in front of me. I imagined touching it, letting the soft liquid trace through my fingers, energizing every molecule with my intentions.

I felt it.

There was a tiny ounce of connection.

I held on to it as if the water itself was a part of me: my limbs, my fingers, my toes, my mind.

"Shea. Open your eyes." I heard Lucian's voice as if he were miles away.

I did as he asked and couldn't believe what I was seeing.

Before me was a giant cyclone of water over ten feet tall. Small splashes of dirty pond hit my face as the raging vortex spun faster and faster.

I couldn't stop it.

Panic seemed like a good call.

Lucian's arms wrapped around me from behind. His breath was soft on my ear as he whispered, "Just relax and disconnect."

The water swirled wider, out of control. I wanted to run, but feeling the strength of his arms gave me power from within.

I stared at the inverted whirlpool. *I'd* created that.

With sudden clarity, I knew I could bend it to my will. Whatever I wanted to do with it, I could, like it was a part of me.

It *was* a part of me.

With a large sigh, the water collapsed back into the pond. It was still. Not even a ripple.

I turned in his arms, my adrenaline pumping. "I did it!" I cried excitedly.

Apparently, my enthusiasm made me irresistible because before I could utter another word he was kissing me. After what I'd just accomplished, the energy that surged through me only fueled the fire, and before I knew it, Lucian was carrying me back inside.

Even though this had happened every day for the last three months, I still had butterflies. Being with Lucian was like nothing I could put into words. Every touch made me blind with desire. Every kiss felt like the first time.

We were made for each other.

He carefully set me down on our bed, his hands never leaving my body. Wrapping my arms around him, I drew him in closer, wanting to feel the heat of his chest against mine. Being with him was so powerful I found myself gasping for air.

My head floated in the clouds as we made love.

***

"What is it, your nap time? It's only two thirty in the afternoon, or is it later?" Aidan stood before me in a forest.

I was Dream-Walking.

I must have dozed off after being with Lucian. The boy

zonked me out.

Lucky me.

Aidan always brought me a rush of happiness. Seeing him there with his big blue eyes, messy brown hair, and abs for days, I reached up to his six-foot frame and gave him the biggest hug I could muster.

I pulled away with a huge grin, which he returned in kind. His eyes sparkled with an inner kindness that always took my breath away.

"Yes, smart-ass," I answered. "It's two thirty in the afternoon, and maybe I just wanted to see you. Is that so wrong?" I nudged him affectionately. Looking around at all the trees, I had to ask, "Where is this place?"

"In the Angeles Forest, just outside Los Angeles." Then, in a quick change of mood, Aidan's face turned serious. "I think I'm close."

He didn't have to say what he was close to.

Aidan had been hunting Caelius since he'd escaped three months ago. I'd been Dream-Walking with him to stay up-to-date on the situation, and to visit because Aidan was more than just my best friend. We'd been born on the same day, minute, and second for a reason. I was called a Vessel. And Aidan was one of four remaining brothers who protected the Light, which I was apparently made out of. Yeah, it didn't sound crazy at all!

He'd been sent down in human form to protect me from, well, Lucian. Before we'd known we were made for each other, Lucian's job had been to hunt down Vessels to help free his father, Caelius, from where he'd been imprisoned. "Help" may have been the wrong word; draining my soul until the prison cracked open was more like it.

Once Lucian had realized his feelings for me, he'd flat-out refused to take me, but Lucian's first son, Ur-Nammu, had kidnapped me and taken me there anyway, hence Caelius's "get out of jail free card." Luckily, he hadn't finished the ritual, which would've ended up sucking out my soul and restoring him to full power. But Caelius had still managed to drain enough of my Light to escape.

It was all a big mess, but I trusted Aidan with my life.

Even though he'd stabbed me in the gut.

One would think my trust might have wavered at that point, and, I'll admit, it had for a little while. But I understood his decision. His brothers believed that if Caelius was freed it would mean the end of the world as we knew it. Since I was the key to opening his prison, it was better to destroy the key than risk the chance of Caelius obliterating the planet.

It made sense, so I understood the "why" of his actions. Still, the emotional betrayal of my best friend had been far worse than the knife he'd twisted in my gut. But when Aidan had showed up with Lucian to save me from Caelius, I'd seen in his eyes that he would never hurt me again.

It was hard to explain, but my loyalty to Aidan was even fiercer than before. There was something about finding out I was an elemental created from Light—a Light the beast-brothers had protected since the dawn of time—that put the matter into perspective.

"Caelius in Los Angeles?" I rolled my eyes. I was actually surprised he hadn't gone to Las Vegas. The irony would've been that much sweeter.

Aidan gave a chuckle. "Right?" His face turned contemplative. "I'm just not sure what he's doing here. The whole time I've been tracking Caelius, I keep getting the feeling he's tracking someone as well, but it's not you or Lucian."

"Or you," I added.

"Or me," he conceded. "Lucian is Caelius's *only* son. Why wouldn't he want to find him and convince him to come back to the fold?"

"Maybe he's pissed. I mean, Lucian did align himself with you and your brothers and try to kill him." That last battle in Caelius's cell had been brutal: five against one with me in the mix. I hadn't thought the monster had a chance in hell of surviving. But one moment the boys had been tearing the vampire to shreds, and the next he was gone and the curse was broken.

I'd felt something brush up against me. In hindsight I now knew it'd been Caelius. If I'd figured it out, I could have stopped him. But I'd let him slip right past me . . .

I shook my head from the memory. I needed to focus on the here and now.

"Caelius didn't know anybody before Lucian, right?" I asked aloud. "I mean, wasn't he 'Darkness incarnate' before he decided to take human form? Lucian is the only one he met who's still alive."

Aidan shrugged. "I thought it might be Ur-Nammu Caelius is hunting, but that vamp is in Miami."

"Miami?" The image of Ur-Nammu sunbathing on Miami Beach popped into my head, and I couldn't stop from laughing. "That's the last place I'd imagine him going."

Aidan smiled, but it was a hollow smile; he didn't find it that funny, which made the hairs on my neck rise.

"Miami is no joke, Shea. It used to be a nighttime feast for vampires down there, what with the party scene, but now that they're active during the day, the missing person reports are piling up. Ur-Nammu is probably there on Caelius's orders to punish a few of the overzealous vampires. Caelius wants to be the main show; he doesn't want his 'diluted grandchildren' stealing the spotlight. Until he gets his power back, he wants his kind to live in secret. If there are to be mass killings, Caelius will want all the credit . . ." Aidan's expression took on a far-off look.

"You have thinky-face. What is it?" I asked.

"Nothing. I just thought of something. I might know who Caelius is after." Aidan didn't look pleased.

"Who?" For some reason I didn't want to know. Aidan's expression said it all. Whoever papa-vampire was after, it wasn't good.

Aidan grimaced. "I don't want to say. Just hope that I'm wrong."

"I'll definitely do that. Your face is freaking me out." I cringed.

Apparently, not wanting to worry me further, he smiled, trying to ease the tension. "So, how's your training going?"

I had to brag. "I made a whirlpool."

Aidan nodded his head, impressed. "That's really good. You're getting stronger."

Then I added with a bang, "I made it in the air, sucker!"

His eyes widened. "Holy crap, are you serious?"

"It was ginormous! It looked like a water tornado!" Okay, yeah, I was proud of myself.

"That's amazing!" His eyes were still wide. "No Vessel has

14

been this powerful this quick. Even Moses took years to learn his strengths. Maybe it's because you're the last one."

"Or, like I've told you over and over, it's because I'm a girl, which on principal makes me better," I teased. All the Vessels before me had been men. I was the first female.

Aidan's eyes did all the smiling for me.

"I can't argue with your logic," he said with a laugh. "Still, you'd better wake up, lazy butt. Tell Lucian where I am, and be careful." He was suddenly full of concern.

"I will, but you be more careful. Contact me as soon as you find Caelius. Don't be a hero. We need to confront him together." I sounded like a mom.

Aidan didn't seem to mind. He reached down and gave me another hug. "Love you."

"Love you too," I said into his chest.

***

I woke up to see the sun slowly setting through the window. It was almost as stunning as Lucian lying beside me. He watched me with his usual mixture of love, desire, and concern.

"I just talked to Aidan," I said at last, breaking the silence.

Concern won out. "Did he find Caelius?" Then, as if he didn't want to ask, he added, "Is Aidan okay?"

The bromance between Lucian and Aidan was pretty adorable to me, but I'd only witnessed the tail end of their long history. The first Vessel had been Moses. Yes, *Moses*, and he'd bonded the two of them like family. When Aidan had thought Lucian was going to take Moses to Caelius, he'd killed Moses.

15

It was only recently that Lucian had forgiven Aidan. Lucian had made it his mission to torture him with every Vessel after Moses. He'd wanted him to suffer as he had suffered after losing them. Boys and their grudges. Aidan definitely hadn't deserved what Lucian had done to him over the centuries, but I wasn't about to get in the middle of that can of worms.

I guessed I was the one who'd brought the two of them together again after all those years. I could tell there was still some tension between them, but the love was there too. I didn't want to interfere, so I'd decided to stand back and let them figure it out on their own.

"Aidan is fine. He's just outside of Los Angeles," I said.

"Los Angeles? Why there?" Lucian asked.

"He thinks Caelius is tracking someone. He has an idea who, but won't tell me," I confessed.

"Ur-Nammu?"

I shook my head. "I thought the same thing, but Ur-Nammu's in Miami."

Lucian nodded in understanding. "That was always a cesspool of vampire filth." He reached out his arms and pulled me into him. My head rested comfortably on his chest as I aimlessly traced my finger in slow circles over his necklace. "Los Angeles? I don't know anyone there, so how could Caelius?"

"Maybe someone is hiding there?" I suggested.

Lucian's body tensed.

I kissed his neck, trying to distract him. "We'll have to wait for Aidan to tell us."

The phone rang.

We froze. I didn't even know we had a phone. I wanted to say it was probably a wrong number, but I knew it was Aidan.

If he was calling, then he couldn't wait for me to fall asleep.

My eyes met Lucian's.

"It's Aidan," he said.

I nodded. "I'll get it."

"No." Lucian gracefully stepped out of bed. He walked over to the phone that was apparently on the desk in our room. "Aidan—"

His voice caught.

That scared me more than anything.

I couldn't hear Aidan, but whatever he was saying made Lucian's skin pale.

He hung up the phone, and his eyes filled with anguish as he whispered one word.

"Gracuri."

CHAPTER 2
LUCIAN

Shea kept asking me questions, her tone panicked, but I couldn't hear her. I couldn't hear anything but a slight ringing.

These past months with her had been a dream—a dream I didn't want to wake from. It was as if Caelius had killed us all in that cave, and I'd died and ended up with Shea in this bliss. Granted I was no fool and needed to prepare her, but I didn't care. I didn't want to care.

Caelius and *his* world, with all his wants and needs and commands, had been my burden for over three thousand years. The weight of his power breaking and twisting me in new ways every century, the torment of torturing Aidan and killing the Vessel . . . I'd become more monster than man.

But with Shea I felt like I had in Gutium before the wars. I was finally free from the burdens of my past.

I'd hoped Caelius would just destroy the world, that it'd be swift, and that I'd be making love to Shea when it happened.

I knew that was idealistic. If Aidan or Shea were to discover my intent, they'd be furious: furious in a way one child is with another, not in the way Caelius was. They didn't understand him. They hadn't been exposed to his unfathomable rage for as long as I had. Even Aidan was blind to Caelius's *true* power.

I'd been inside him. I'd touched the center of his madness, the black hole that consumed all reason. I had become *nothing*. Everything I'd identified with—my memories, my homeland, everything that made me, that gave me reason, even my very soul—had all disappeared.

I'd never imagined a place like that existed. The lure of hell was something I scoffed at; being tormented by Caelius was hell. But that cold, dark, empty place at the center of his being . . . the nothingness . . . I'd rather be strapped to a stalagmite and have him ravage me over and over than to feel that way again.

I closed my eyes, breathing in deep. Now I felt it, the shame of what I'd been doing. In truth, I was afraid.

Shea's soft arms wrapped around my body, her concern flowing over her small frame. She pressed her head into my chest, whispering, "Whatever it is, we'll get through it together."

I sighed with regret. Who was I kidding? I hadn't been training Shea, I'd been hiding her, hoping death or bliss would take us, hoping she would never have to feel Caelius's emptiness. What if he consumed her soul and I lost her forever?

I opened my eyes and pulled back to look at her face, running my hand along the soft line of her cheekbone. "I don't want him to hurt you. This is my fault. I wasn't thinking. I should have separated myself from you and let you train with Aidan. It's my responsibility to keep my children safe. It's my responsibility to handle Caelius. I can't—"

"Are you freaking kidding me right now?" Her tone was sharp. I hadn't heard Shea use that edge since we'd first met.

I tilted my head. "Why don't you just add 'dorm monitor' to the end of that?"

Shea's eyes softened. "What I meant was that's enough of you blaming yourself. And I'm here with you because I want to be. I don't want to think about you dropping me off with Aidan and disappearing. I mean, how could you even say that?"

I reached down, kissing the small of her neck. "It's not that, Shea. Caelius is drawing me out. There's very little I care about in this world, only a handful of people: you, Aidan, and my Second-Borns—Ur-Nammu, Gracuri, Duncan, Bohe, and David—if they're still alive. I trust that Gracuri hid them well. He was probably leading Caelius away from them. He'd do anything for the one he loves, and so would I."

I stared into her, seeing the core of all I'd longed to protect, and it was killing me.

She stroked my arm, looking deep into my eyes. "Where are you right now?"

I grabbed Shea's wrist. "It's too dangerous. He knows we're together, and all of this could be a trap to get to you. He could use me to hurt you, Shea!"

She tried to pry her wrist away. "You're the only one hurting me right now."

I let go, looking at my own hand in shock. My teeth were bared. I turned away. "I'm sorry, I just . . . he can't have you."

Shea ran her fingertips over my chest. It sent chills through my mind, softening the razor-edged nerves that Caelius always brought out inside me.

"I know. I'm *yours*." Shea smiled. "But we can face whatever that a-hole has for us together."

I combed my hands through her hair, resting my forehead on hers. I could stay like this. If there was a heaven, it was in Shea Harper's arms.

I sighed heavily. She didn't understand. It was too risky, and she wasn't ready . . . because of me.

The smart thing would be to wait it out. I should let Caelius kill Gracuri and use that time to train Shea. Odds were Caelius had already bled him dry.

My stomach churned, thinking about Gracuri's severed head on a spike the way Caelius had ordered it all those years ago. I couldn't take it. He was *my* child. *Mine* to protect. And he was loyal. He was . . . irreplaceable.

Sentiment was clouding my vision. Shea couldn't risk her life for one of my children. She'd gladly do it—she and Aidan both—and that was what Caelius would be expecting. He'd want an audience.

It was a trap, any fool could see that, but I couldn't leave Gracuri to die. No doubt the agonies he'd already endured would scar him forever. I'd promised him. When I'd fed on Gracuri to charge up to face Caelius, I'd given him my word.

I kissed her lips. Shea pulled back for a moment, unsure of what my affection meant. I half smiled, cupping her face in my hands. "You're right. We'll rest tonight. Dream-Walk with Aidan and tell him we'll all meet together outside of LA tomorrow." Then I winked, adding a playful undertone to my voice. "But from here on out, I want you to take your training seriously."

Shea put a hand on her hip, eyeing me suspiciously. "I have been taking this seriously! You'll see, tomorrow I'll obliterate Caelius, and then we'll have the rest of our lives to just enjoy ourselves!"

Finally my enlarged incisors retracted. I smiled a human smile with flat, white teeth. "That sounds like a plan." I kissed her hard. It ached in me, the desire for her to fill my bones, to heal the emptiness with which Caelius had infused my soul.

I ran my fingertips down the small of her back, letting my mouth linger on the curve of her neck. She smelled like warm sunlight, like a rose just before it bloomed.

I dragged my lips up to the soft spot behind her ear. Pulling my hand to the nape of her neck, I grabbed a handful of her hair and pulled, her back arching in response. Shea gasped. It thrilled me, and so did the vibration of her heartbeat against my chest.

I kissed her, and she moaned.

Her sounds could penetrate all reason.

I laid her softly onto the bed, hovering for a moment over her frame. Her eyes were alight with passion, her chest heaving forward.

I needed her.

I knew then that I'd *always* need her. Poets for centuries had mused about touching the surface of the sun; they'd tried in muddied words to express the bliss, pain, and fulfillment of finding your soulmate. Now they seemed just words, hollow things that would never equate to the truth and beauty held in her eyes.

I leaned my hips heavily onto hers. "I love you, Shea. No matter what happens." Before she could respond, I swept inside her. Our bodies fused like blood in water.

I held her wrists, thrusting as she bit my lip and wrapped her thighs around my back. I growled instinctually and pushed harder. Her nails ran down my sides, and the marks healed as she moved. Tears welled in her eyes, and she whispered into my ear, "I'll love you forever, Lucian."

It broke me. I didn't know that I could ache for someone while being this close. It was like when she'd burned out a piece of my rib cage. Shea's words would always leave a mark that time could not erase, a hole that could only be filled by more of her, her love, her touch.

Hours passed until she fell asleep from exhaustion.

Good.

I needed her to sleep through the night.

It might give me enough time.

She slept with a slight smile on her face. Shea was transparent that way. It was so rare. I wavered. What was I doing? This could be the last time I saw her. And for whom? Gracuri?

My insides twisted again. Gracuri had been there for me. It was because of him that I hadn't killed myself looking for Shea. That pile of bodies. I shivered, the guilt gnawing at me. That had been *his* solution, but it had saved me. It was his blood that had given me the strength to stand against Caelius. Caelius had no doubt smelled it on me. I was sure he'd tortured Gracuri to madness for that alone.

I may have been a monster who didn't deserve Shea, but I wasn't a coward. I was still Gutian, and Gutians didn't leave the ones they loved to die.

I had fought against my own maker—against Caelius—for

Shea, for my very soul. I'd earned the heavy weight of the code of my people standing beside her, and now I couldn't go back to being calloused.

I couldn't abandon Gracuri and what he meant to me. I may have been a poet and craftsman as a young boy, but today I was more the warrior my father deserved than ever before.

I gently left Shea's side and walked to the balcony, surveying the outside. I'd done perimeter checks nightly while she slept. There was no sign of vampires near the villa—I'd made sure of that. She was safe here.

I leapt into the cold sky. I flew over countries and crossed the ocean. When I came to California, it was barely morning, the sun just rising over the mountains. It was breathtaking. I'd never seen Los Angeles lit up like this in daylight. I almost felt human, seeing all the people below, driving their cars, heading to work, loading children into minivans while staring at a strange floating man in the sky.

I was used to traveling at night: no eyes, no onlookers. I meshed with darkness. In daylight I'd have to be more careful. I shook my head, running my hands through my thick black hair. I was never this careless. Already Caelius had an advantage. I flew quickly to the Angeles Forest.

When I landed, I walked among the trees, picking up the scent of Gracuri's blood. Words rattled through my head from the last time we had spoken. *I can't thank you enough, Gracuri. You saved my other children from slaughter, you saved my life, and because you exposed us again, Caelius will no doubt demand your head.* I clenched my hands into fists.

My hope was that Caelius had kept him mostly intact,

wanting to wait so that I would have to watch his torture.

The tip of my boot tapped something soft—a severed hand. My shoulders sagged, and I sighed heavily. I eyed the trail of dismembered body parts. The woods were drenched with blood. It was thrown everywhere. Wasted. For sport.

I stepped back, shaking with emotion as my mind tried to steady itself. I extended my senses, feeling for Caelius. I rose from the ground slowly, hovering over the grass. The vow I had given Gracuri with such confidence screamed through my mind. *I promise, I will defend you with my last breath.*

I heard a cry, a ghastly and twisted scream that shook my bones. I'd never heard Gracuri make that sound before. Not in Athens, nor in Thebes when he'd gouged out his own eyes. Even then, his agonizing wail had been nothing like this.

I vomited, or at least I tried to. My whole body heaved, but nothing came out. I didn't have a stomach with acid in it anymore. When I drank blood, it absorbed into every cell of my body. There was nothing to pump, but the reflex kept me gagging.

I closed my eyes. *Gracuri, what has he done to you?* My fears were accompanied by the realization that I hadn't fed. I was coming to this battle weak. My concern had driven me relentlessly here, ignoring everything I'd learned battling with Adnachiel over the centuries.

"Please!" Gracuri cried. His anguish pierced me like a piece of glass through my stomach. I flew desperately to the sound of his cries. It didn't matter if I wasn't ready; he needed me *now.*

My own words played over and over in my mind. The look in those baby-blue eyes after he'd fed from me. The need. The

25

unconditional belief when I'd said, *I promise . . . he will never have you.*

I panted for breath, covering miles in moments. Branches and pine needles tore away strips of flesh as I hurtled forward.

Gracuri.

My stomach heaved again. The thought of his dismemberment, of what I was about to see, was agonizing. The Gutian code of my people and my promise to him rang like white noise when I reached the sound of his wails, taking in Caelius's masterpiece at last.

Gracuri deserved better than this.

He was propped up on display. His wrists and ankles were chained between two giant oak trees with chains that stretched out and wrapped like a web through the woods.

I trembled.

Around Gracuri lay bloodied spikes and a whip encrusted with nails and barbs, torture devices from the Middle Ages that Caelius must have stolen from museums.

From the flayed way Gracuri looked, this ordeal had been going on for some time, long before Aidan had told Shea about his suspicions. My own words hit me again. *He'll never have you.*

I moved to stand in front of Gracuri, inches from his face. My smell awoke his blood. He looked up quickly. Tears streamed down his cheeks while he shook his head no.

I reached up to the shackle on his left arm and crushed it. As I did, fury filled the emptiness in that part of my mind still belonging to Caelius. That monster had done this just to prove that he could.

I crushed the other shackle, and Gracuri collapsed into my

26

arms. His knees buckled. He was double my size, but I picked him up easily, holding him like a child.

His lips trembled. "No, please. Father, you can't be here! Go, now!"

"I won't leave you." I rested his head against my chest, tears welling in my eyes at seeing him so torn to pieces. It was grotesque what Caelius had done to his once powerful frame. Grotesque and my fault.

I leapt into the air and flew, keeping his body pressed tenderly against my own, his name repeating in my mind like the beat of a soft drum: Gracuri. Gracuri. Gracuri.

I'd make it up to him somehow. I'd never let any of my children drink from me after I'd turned them, but maybe just this once, for Gracuri.

Once we were safe and I could hide him away, I'd offer him the blood he'd begged for in his youth. I owed him that much and more.

I moved my hand through his matted wisps of curly hair, comforting his jagged breath. We'd slept like this when he'd first turned and was unsure of the new world around him. "You're safe now. I have you."

I flew toward the desert as fast and as hard as I could.

"Why didn't you call out for me? All you had to do was say my name, and I would have known where you were. I could have saved you from this."

He wept into my arms. "Please, just leave me and go. He can't have you, not for me. Please—"

A spike of pain seared into my body like fire. It was worse than the burning lava of Pompeii. I plummeted like a rock to the desert below.

I wrapped my arms around Gracuri, trying to break our fall with my body. It was no use. When I landed, he broke loose from me, his body flying out of sight.

I coughed, writhing on the ground. Reaching my hand to the back of my neck, I pulled out a long wooden stake, which had plunged all the way through, crushing my spine.

Blood poured out of the wound. I couldn't get up. I couldn't feel my body.

Gracuri screamed.

Within moments, white shoes were inches from me—a pile of long spikes held together by barbed wire dragging behind them. They were Gracuri's shoes. I followed the legs up to Caelius's face.

He smiled. "Lucian. It's so good to see you, my son."

Leaning down, Caelius ran a long finger through my hair. "You fly quicker than I would have expected. I was hoping we could play this little game out in the forest, but you are a fan of *deserts*, aren't you?" He stood up, surveying the empty plain. "Isn't this near where you met your blessed Shea Harper? Arizona? Shall we infuse it with some new memories . . . *better* ones?"

Wind moved through the gaping hole in my throat. Just hearing him say Shea's name was infuriating. I couldn't think, I had to move. I struggled to rise.

Caelius shook his head, leaning down over my wincing frame. "I can't have you go slithering off, Son. I've got a show for you, and I've been waiting patiently for this moment." He rammed the long, pole-like stakes from the pile behind him through my hands, arms, and chest.

I screamed in agony, but nothing came out but a wheezing

sound: air forcing its way out through the gaping hole in my throat.

I gritted my teeth. Why was he wearing Gracuri's shoes? I couldn't turn my head but darted my eyes. Where was he?

Caelius touched my neck wound tenderly. "That was a close one. A bit over and I would have lopped off your head. It's a good thing I'm an excellent shot." The fingernail on his hand grew long and sharp, then he cut a thin line down my cheek, drawing blood. With pleasure, he slowly licked the bloody fingernail. "How *dare* you bring me to this, Lucian. You know I would be lost without you, my precious son. Your taste alone . . . there is no other I long for."

I spat, but it barely made it past my own mouth. My cervical vertebra was severely damaged, partially severed: a critical hit to any vampire. The wood had also splintered off into my bones. I struggled, but it was no use. I couldn't move.

My blood was currently being lapped up by the dry desert underneath me. Its thirst and mine grew with every drop.

But it didn't matter.

Nothing mattered but finding Gracuri and getting him away from here.

If he was smart, he'd run the instant he broke free of my arms. And if he was a fool, I hoped that any one of the Greek gods he prayed to would have mercy and save him.

I glanced briefly at Gracuri's white shoes. When I'd found him he'd been barefoot, naked, bloodied, and ravaged. But the shoes Caelius wore were clean and stark white. He'd prepared for this, unlike I had.

I tried to move and panted from the exertion, my body

struggling to respond. I was pinned apart like a mounted taxidermic butterfly.

Caelius gazed down at me with pleasure. "Now for the show." In a flash he was gone. When he returned, he had Gracuri on his knees. Caelius held him up by his curly hair, his long nails sinking into Gracuri's neck as he taunted me. "I asked my son to bring me your head, Gracuri, and he didn't. If he'd beheaded you *then*, you would've been saved from all this torture. You have your father to thank for this prolonged death."

Gracuri's lips moved, but the sound was soft, weak.

My lips mouthed the words I wanted to shout at him. "Fool! You should have run!"

My mind reeled. I wasn't sure if I thought he was a fool or that I was for believing there was any holy mercy set aside for anyone who had come to care for me.

Caelius laughed. "Come, now, we can't hear you, Gracuri. Project. From the diaphragm."

I couldn't stand it. I screamed in anger, ripping the bone of my arm through one of the spikes. Gracuri's eyes swelled with tears as his torn voice pushed out the words, "I'm so sorry, Lucian. I didn't want you to save me. No matter what Caelius says, I don't blame you. You're my world."

Caelius pulled Gracuri up to his feet, then wrapped his arms around his waist as he licked his neck victoriously. "You could learn something from this sack of meat, Lucian. *He* is loyal to his father. I devoured his children in front of him, one by one. I tortured and dismembered his favorites. And he remained *loyal* to you, even when it hurt. *Loyal*. Still, I loved watching him cry. It's rare, isn't it, tears for our kind?"

I gurgled as blood filled my mouth and my body convulsed. Caelius pulled Gracuri's eyelids open and shoved him forward. "Watch now, you pathetic excuse for a vampire. Watch as Lucian's body turns against him. He should die and revive, like you did a hundred times, but he won't. Look at his wounds. Aren't they greater and more severe than what you've suffered? Every bone in his body is broken, lanced."

Gracuri tried to jerk free, to reach for me, but Caelius held him tight. I gasped, fighting death. I always resisted it when Caelius was having his "fun." I closed my eyes and gritted my teeth until the moment passed.

When my eyes opened, Caelius laughed, dropping Gracuri to the earth like a rag doll. He crawled over to me on his hands and knees. He tried to pull out one of the spikes but was too debilitated. I looked into his eyes, sending my thoughts through him. *Gracuri, leave! I owe so much to you, let me give you this chance. I'll distract Caelius. Just run. Run, now! Save yourself and let me make good on my promise.*

He shook his head no, and Caelius laughed further.

"You see, Gracuri, the moment of death came for Lucian, but did he give into it? No. He fought the agony and held on. It's a wonder, isn't it? It would be easier to simply allow his weak body to die, then let his vampire blood, *my* blood, revive him. But he won't do it! You can imagine the things I've done to him, but he just hates, no, *despises* going to that dark, empty place of death. Which is our *home!*"

Caelius scowled as he leaned down and sat between us. He played with Gracuri's hair, lacing it between his fingertips, boredom overtaking his features.

31

Gracuri winced, pulling his head back in shame. When his eyes met mine, they were again filled with tears, but Caelius continued on. "That's why he's different, my Lucian. Better. Although I can't condone some of his choices. He seems attracted to mice, to rodents lower than him. Maybe it makes him feel more like a god to have pathetic servants like you and Shea around to grovel at his feet."

I moved my bloodied fingertip to Gracuri's. My pointer barely touched his thumb.

I pushed past the rips in my throat, forcing sound. It was barely a whisper, but something our kind could hear. "Why won't you just leave?" I pleaded. If he wouldn't listen to my mind, then maybe my words could reach him. I needed him to live. I needed him.

"Because he loves you, you fool! That's why he won't just leave you here!" Caelius shouted, his eyes black as night as his incisors grew to the shape of thick talons.

I struggled, pulling against the stakes as Caelius stood up. He grabbed Gracuri by the neck and held him in the air. "I tortured him for months, yet he wouldn't cry out for you! He wouldn't draw you to me! I finally had to leave a fuming trail for that dog, Adnachiel, to follow. Do you know how frustrating that was, waiting for you, my son? I had to tolerate his filth to draw you out. And how predictable. I'm sure you rushed over as soon as you caught wind of Gracuri's capture."

"Let him go, Caelius." A fourth voice joined us. I couldn't see his face, but I recognized the tone.

Aidan.

He stepped beside my mutilated frame.

I coughed, ripping another spike through my leg, freeing it in shreds. "Aidan, get out of here!" I screamed, but my voice came out as a whisper. I couldn't lose them both.

He knelt beside me, his eyes full of compassion. "Shea told me what you said. I thought I would scout ahead before we met up. When I saw Gracuri was gone, I knew you were involved."

"Did you tell her?" I choked.

Shea.

This was exactly what I'd been trying to avoid: lining up everyone I loved, all to be slaughtered, all so Caelius could revel in my agonies.

He stood up without answering.

The air was still as Caelius eyed his tall frame. I ripped another spike from the side of my torso as Gracuri's voice broke the silence. "I'm sorry, Father. I didn't want Caelius to use me against you. I would have rather died! I tried to . . . I tried to experience true death so many times. But he revived me." His voice came out in sobs, and I ached to comfort him.

"Always remember what I said to you when we first met in Thebes. I will always feel that way about you, Lucian. You've kept the deal we made then. Please don't blame your—"

Before Aidan had a chance to move, Caelius had sunk his teeth into Gracuri.

I cried out.

Aidan lunged at Caelius with his bare hands, but it was too late. Caelius flew into the air, toward the sun.

Aidan scrambled at the empty space where they'd been. His large invisible wing was useless, the other just a flapping nub from where Caelius had ripped it out the last time we'd faced him.

"Get these spikes out!" I screamed savagely, my fangs growing as they cut my lips.

Aidan rushed to me, pulling out the stakes as gently as possible. "Just tear them apart, there's no time!" I shouted.

He complied, cracking my bones as he threw the spikes miles into the air, toward where Caelius had disappeared.

I ripped my foot free of the last one, separating my arch into what looked like two giant toes.

I forced myself to stand.

Before I could leap into the air, Gracuri's voice reached my ears, a faint whisper carried on the wind. "We'll walk by the river together again. Hand in hand, like we used to. I'll see you again one day. I will always love—"

Gracuri's headless body landed by my feet.

My eyes widened in horror.

It was emaciated and drained.

"No . . ." I staggered. Aidan reached out to help me. I jerked from his grasp, hurtling my body into the sky.

The last thing I heard was the distant sound of his voice screaming out for me to wait.

It didn't matter.

I was blind with fury.

Gracuri.

Gracuri.

Gracuri.

His name had been a comfort just a few minutes ago. It had rolled like a drum in my head as I'd caressed his Greek curls. This couldn't be happening. I'd promised him. I'd had him in my arms. That wasn't his body. Caelius was just toying with me. He wasn't dead!

I broke free of the cloud cover, piercing it in a torrent of wind that howled in waves behind me.

Caelius was hovering in the air, nonchalantly licking his red mouth as he held Gracuri's head on a spike.

I screamed a sound so savage and animallike that Caelius jerked back, caught off guard. I lunged toward him, baring my fangs. I pushed him toward the earth with the force of a meteor.

When our bodies hit the ground, the desert cracked open and dirt mounded like a tidal wave around us. I ripped at Caelius's face, his chest, splattering his blood across the sand. But it wasn't his blood. It was Gracuri's blood *in* him.

I had to get it out.

Every drop of it.

Gracuri wasn't his.

Wasn't his to kill.

Wasn't his to *own*.

He tossed my body into a patch of cactus. The thorns stuck out in every direction, impaling me, but I didn't care. What was pain now that I'd lost him? I called the snakes. Rattlers moved out of their holes and slithered by my feet as I walked toward Caelius.

He smiled, pleased. The gashes on his body from my attack healed before my eyes. Having drunk a Second-Born, he was radiating power. "I love this, don't you? You're like a cub trying out his bite and growl on his father. Don't worry, Lucian. My hide is thick. I can take it."

I bared my fangs and hissed. Under my command, the ocean

of snakes slithered forward to cover his body. Some he struck away, but most of them bit hard and sank in their venom. It would have been enough to cause paralysis in a powerful vampire, but Caelius brushed them off lightly and wiggled his body as if they were feathers tickling his back.

I sneered. "I'm not *practicing* on you. My rage is not *yours*. It's *mine*! Just like Gracuri was *mine*! And his death—"

"Was *yours*!" Caelius shouted, stepping toward me. He crushed a dozen rattlers' heads with his feet as he closed the distance between us. "Gracuri's death was because of *you*. Why do you think I sought him out first?"

He was close to me now; I didn't shrink back. Caelius ran his hand down the side of my cheek as hot tears covered his fingertips.

I wasn't standing; I could only hover above the earth. My bones were all broken—they couldn't bear my weight. Ferocity had given me power, momentary strength.

Caelius smiled, eyeing my weakness. "When will you learn that nothing you have is yours? *My* blood running through you makes everyone you touch *mine*! Even that whore, Shea."

Before I could rip out his throat, he pinned me down against the hot dirt. Sitting on my torso, he gleefully swatted my face. I spat blood in every direction. When Caelius stopped, I could barely see him through the red streams flowing from my bleeding forehead.

He ground his hips into mine as he licked the side of my neck, furthering my humiliation. "My sweet boy. Still so headstrong." He sank his teeth into my neck, drinking my blood. I pushed against his chest, but I felt my strength becoming his. He'd never been able to drink me in shadow form. Other than the day Caelius had turned me, I'd never felt him suck me down.

Everything slowed.

"Stop. That's enough." A blurry figure stood behind us.

Caelius pulled back, growling. "Of course that's enough! He has *one* drop of my blood left in him, keeping his body animated. Close to comatose, but alive. He *is* alive."

I coughed, the light blinding me. As Caelius let me go, my head thudded to the earth.

He stood up, walking toward the hazy figure. My body was shutting down. This was the closest I'd come to *true* death. It felt like the night Caelius had taken me in Egypt, when I'd died in my mortal flesh. Now I would die a vampire. Without Caelius's blood in my veins, I wouldn't revive.

"Will he survive?" The figure seemed concerned.

"Of course, he has one drop. What do you think of me?" Caelius spat out in reply.

That voice. It was female and familiar. My mind filled with terror. Shea?

I rolled to my side and reached for her. "Shea, get out of here, you're not ready!"

Arms instantly wrapped around my frame and held me tenderly. She kissed my forehead and moved her hand down the side of my face. She smelled of frankincense and myrrh.

I squinted, the light behind her shadowing her face. I couldn't be certain. "Shea?"

She didn't answer.

"Shea, you have to leave me."

She placed her finger over my mouth and addressed Caelius.

"He's delirious. He thinks I'm the Vessel."

Caelius scoffed. "To be expected. His mind will recover. We need him weak so that he can remember who his *real* family is. I can giveth, and I can taketh away, Child."

"I've never left you, Lucian." Her voice rumbled like the sound of thunder in my ears. It was powerful and certain. "Ours is a proud people. I could never let you die. I will be by your side always, my love."

My jaw fell slack as my eyes adjusted. I reached my hand up, touching her face in disbelief. What was I seeing? Had I really died? Had Caelius ended me, and was this who would take me down the river of death?

There was a sweetness in her smile like there had been in childhood. "It's been a long time since you've seen me, Lucian. But I've watched over you for centuries."

I gasped, pulling her head closer to mine. "Nefertiti . . . I killed you. It's impossible. I mourned you for thousands of years."

Sadness glossed over her face.

"Um, get your hands off him." *Another* voice?

Nefertiti hissed and pulled back.

I looked up in confusion . . . at Shea and Aidan. My mind fogged. I'd lost too much blood. I couldn't will myself to move. I wasn't sure what was real. If Nefertiti was here, then I was dead. If I was dead, where was Gracuri? Had he not just promised to walk with me by the river when the time came? And what was Shea doing here?

I watched as her eyes surveyed all of my gashes. Her lips trembled in anger. "We should've come together."

I tried to whisper that I was sorry, but my mouth was too dry.

My arm just reached and thudded toward her like empty meat.

She gasped. Aidan grabbed her hand. She looked at him.

Aidan only nodded.

Caelius stood there happily. "Look what you made me do to my son, whore."

I struggled to move. This was the audience he'd been hoping for. With my last bit of strength I shouted, "You've fallen right into his hands! She's not ready yet—get her out of here!" I made eye contact, and Aidan flinched, staring into the fury of my vacant pools.

That was the last of what I had in me. My eyes couldn't stay open. I felt my body lift, and then I felt the force of the wind as everything went black.

CHAPTER 3
SHEA

"**W**here did she take him?" I screamed at smug-faced Caelius. At the moment, I didn't comprehend that he could probably crush me with his mind. I was too surprised that Lucian—who had been lying on the ground, emaciated and half-dead—had been in the arms of some *woman*, and then they'd suddenly been in the air and were gone.

Gone!

With some chick!

Then it hit me.

"Wait. Was that *Nefertiti*?" I yelled at Caelius.

He stared at me, auburn eyes alight with resentment. "You *dare* talk to me in such a tone, you worm? You're not worthy of—"

"Seriously, was that Nefertiti?" I interrupted Vampire Daddy's monologue. I needed to know, and I needed to know *now*. I turned to Aidan.

Aidan looked horrified, as if I'd walked in on him naked. "I . . . never really met her. Yes?" He cringed.

I was frozen in shock.

Not only was Nefertiti alive, but she was a badass vampire who had just *flown* away with Lucian.

My Lucian.

I bet she thought the same thing, that Lucian was *hers*, that he'd been hers for three thousand years. What claim did I have on him? A few lousy months? There was no way he'd pick me over her.

The thought of that struck me in a way that made me want to fall to my knees and cry.

How could Lucian want me when he could have freaking *Nefertiti*?

"You will *not* disrespect me again!" Caelius's voice boomed through the air.

I was so wrapped up in my own agony that it startled me back into my current situation.

The "Master of Darkness" was pretty upset with me.

But what Caelius didn't realize was that I was even more upset with him. He was responsible for Lucian being torn to shreds and drained of a crap-ton of blood. He was practically a living skeleton. Not even during the epic smackdown in Caelius's prison had I seen Lucian like that.

And Jerk Daddy was at fault.

He needed to be taught a lesson.

And it seemed he felt the same way about me.

Caelius threw his hands out to exert some sort of power, and I flinched, expecting *something* to happen.

41

Nothing.

I wanted to laugh. So I did.

This made Caelius even more furious, but before he could speak, I said, perhaps a little smugly, "You can't compel me, so I guess you're kind of screwed." I couldn't help but gloat. Probably a stupid move, but it felt so damn good.

My words were a lot more confident than I actually felt because I was pretty sure that if Caelius got his hands on me, he could tear me apart in less than a second.

As if hearing my thoughts, Caelius flew at me.

Instincts kicked in, and I connected with the earth. We were in Arizona now: my home. It gave me the strength I needed.

Even as Caelius launched himself toward me, sand rose from the ground like a giant funnel, swallowing him whole. I felt like I was in *Dune* controlling the sand worms. I could see Caelius through the maelstrom of swirling dirt as the tiny rocks shredded his skin, and he was smiling.

Caelius ripped out of the sand prison and charged at me again. I wasn't ready for it. I stepped backward, and Aidan tackled him to the ground before he could reach me, his brute strength forcing Caelius down.

But not for long.

Caelius may have been in a weakened state after escaping his prison, but he was still evil incarnate and more than a match for either of us. I knew this, but I needed Caelius to doubt himself. I needed him to believe I could best him.

I needed to make him run away.

As Aidan struggled in his losing battle to keep Caelius down, I searched the area for any signs of life. Being in Arizona, I was hoping for some Joshua trees, but there was nothing in sight except a few scraggly cactuses.

I shrugged. They'd have to do.

But first . . .

I'd figured out pretty quickly back when we fought Caelius down in his pit that he hadn't been around humans in a long time. During that fight, Caelius had put his manipulation skills to the test on Aidan's brothers, trying to convince them the Light was in danger and that they needed to leave. It was plain as day to *me*, but the angels had almost believed him. I knew then that manipulating Caelius would be child's play for a modern-day human.

I was about to try out that theory.

Aidan and Caelius were in a full-on fistfight, which I was grateful no one was around to see, as they had already created a few crater-sized holes in the ground from their impact.

I interrupted the supernatural wrestling match by shouting at Caelius, "You can't hurt me, you know that, right?"

Caelius turned from Aidan to face me. "Is that so?"

But Aidan yanked him back and started pounding on him.

"You're weak, Caelius," I said, taunting him. "You didn't complete the ritual when you escaped. No matter how many people and vamps you drain, you'll never gain your strength." I laughed sarcastically to rub in the lie more deeply. "Even when you were at full power, trapped inside your prison, you still couldn't hurt me. The worst you could do was strip me naked and pretend to rape me while I was unconscious. You know you looked like an idiot, right? When I woke up, I literally gagged. Lucian told me later how he could barely look at you; he was just

43

as disgusted as I was." I cringed. "You're supposed to be someone he looks up to, but you're just a *pervy child molester.*"

Caelius stared at me in rage, his eyes turning pitch-black.

I loved every second of it.

"I'm older than the sands of time, whore. I've seen the birth and death of millions of galaxies. My power is only limited by this weak, pathetic human form. It is the weakness of *your* species that keeps me tethered. And *my* son would never be disgusted by me! Any disgust is only the *human* part of his existence. You can't even comprehend the bond we have."

"I'm just telling you what Lucian told me," I countered, oozing confidence that I didn't have. "He said he wished he'd died when you made him, then he wouldn't have had to live with the embarrassment that you're his father." Oh, I sold it.

Caelius tossed Aidan aside as if he were an annoying bug.

I had just risked everything on this moment.

Connecting to the cactuses, I made them tear through the earth and smash against Caelius full force. And I kept going. I commanded every needle and branch to tear into Caelius's body, ravaging him, shredding him to a pulp.

It wouldn't kill him.

But it rattled him.

His bloody eyes grew round with disbelief.

I was pretty sure I was the only person on record who'd witnessed that phenomenon. Come to think of it, I was pretty sure I was the only one who'd *caused* that phenomenon.

But if I could make Caelius retreat, then Aidan could track him to Lucian.

Every time he tried to break free from the attacking desert

plants, I would add a windstorm of sand and earth to surround him. He choked as his body became a battered mess.

Finally, when he stopped struggling, I released him.

He dropped to the ground.

He was torn up, his skeleton more visible than skin.

I walked over to his writhing body, still terrified but trying my best to look and sound confident. "I could do this all day. You may be able to torture Lucian and your children with your little blood bond, but I'm made from the Light."

Caelius's eyes protruded out of their boney sockets. It was a nightmare staring at his mauled form, but I leaned down until we were face-to-face. "I will end you someday, Caelius, and I'm perfectly happy to make it today."

His voice was ravaged. "You can't kill me."

In a flash, Caelius was gone.

He was so fast, I didn't see him move. One moment Caelius was there, the next only a pile of cactus mush and dirt remained in his place.

I jumped when Aidan put his hand gently on my shoulder.

"Whoa, it's just me. He's gone," he said soothingly. "That was"—he looked around at the debris, his face full of awe—"pretty amazing."

I turned to Aidan, and my knees suddenly gave. He caught me as everything went black.

***

When I woke up, I was lying in a hotel bed with Aidan placing a cold washcloth over my forehead. I sat up, panicked. "Did you

45

track Caelius? I did all of that so you could track him to Lucian!"

Aidan's arms were around me in seconds, trying to calm me down. "Shea, it doesn't work that way. If Caelius doesn't want to be found, I can't find him. My brothers and I thought that once he escaped he'd be trackable, but we were wrong. Caelius *let* me find him with Gracuri. It was all a trap."

A trap.

I knew Aidan was right, but I didn't want to accept it yet. "Why didn't Lucian let me go with him? You saw how I mangled Caelius! I could have saved Gracuri. I could have saved Lucian from . . . her." I couldn't say her name. It hurt too much, especially since Lucian probably didn't want to be saved from Nefertiti. Most likely, he was happy to see her again.

Aidan was having none of it. "If Caelius had stayed one second longer, you would have passed out in front of him, and he could've taken your soul, Shea. Your *soul*. I'd be easy to kill after that. He may be weakened, but he's not weak." Aidan was in full-on scolding mode.

"Okay, *Dad*. I still kicked his butt though," I grumbled.

"You could have died!"

"You wouldn't have let that happen." My voice grew quieter. It was a lame argument. I knew he was right, and there was no way I could justifiably defend myself. I'd acted rashly, and I could have hurt Aidan in the process.

"I might not have had a choice. I'm one angel, and I'm in *human* form. I'm no match for Caelius," he fumed.

Time to grovel.

I hugged him fiercely. "I know, and I'm sorry. I wasn't thinking. But you saw Lucian—he was so ravaged." I shuddered at the memory. "And he was in *her* arms."

I felt Aidan physically relax as he hugged me back. "It was hard for me to see him like that too."

I noticed he didn't mention Nefertiti's name. He was sparing me the agony of having someone else talk about her. It was just like Aidan to be so thoughtful.

He pulled out of the hug to look at me, his face plastered with a huge grin. "Those were some pretty crazy mind games you played on Caelius. I didn't know you had it in you."

I smiled back. "I think I tapped into the fantasy fights part of my brain. You know, where you imagine what you'd say to someone who's bullied you or something. I've had a lot of imaginary conversations with myself. This was the first time I had the balls to say it out loud though."

"Well, it worked. Caelius looked furious. Lucian would be thrilled." Aidan beamed with pride.

But at the mention of Lucian, my heart squeezed.

Aidan saw my face. "Sorry. I'll start trying to find them. Maybe I can find Lucian somehow. I know his presence better than anyone. Who knows, I may get lucky. You stay here."

"First off, no way. Second off, where is *here*?"

"Some generic motel off the highway. We're in Phoenix." I noticed how Aidan deflected my argument for him not to leave without me.

Phoenix. We were close to home, and I missed my parents terribly. Part of me really wanted to pop in and say hello since I could only imagine how worried they were. No word from me for months. Gone from campus. Gone from Arizona. Gone from their lives.

These thoughts must have been written all over my face because Aidan said softly, "You don't have to worry about your parents. We moved them to another city, and my brothers wiped their memories of us completely."

I stood up in shock. "They did *what*?" They had no memory, as if I'd never existed: all the love, my childhood, my life. All of that was gone. It hurt worse than anything.

My parents were the only ones who knew me, who remembered me as the Shea Harper I wanted to be again someday. I wanted to go back to my old life after Caelius was destroyed. I wanted to marry Lucian and have my dad walk me down the aisle. I wanted all those things. Now they were gone forever because beast-boys decided to play God?

Aidan took my hands in his and forced eye contact. "Shea, it's for their own safety and yours too, and it's not forever. If we somehow make it through all this, we can give them their memories back. Just think of the memories as repressed and replaced with new ones. They would have reported you missing, then it would have been even easier for Caelius and his lackeys to find you. We had to protect you."

I shrugged his hands away. "I can protect myself, and I'm going with you to find Lucian. I'm the best weapon you have against Caelius, and you know it." I had to admit, it did make me feel a little better knowing that my parents hadn't lost me forever. It just made me more determined to defeat Caelius so I could get them back.

Aidan couldn't argue against that, but I knew he'd try. "It's too dangerous. You're too valuable."

"Too valuable for what? Caelius has already broken out of his supernatural jail!"

"You know he still needs your soul to gain his full power," Aidan argued. "You're not going, and that's final." Aidan crossed his arms defiantly.

"And who's going to stop me?" I crossed mine as well.

Aidan sighed knowingly. "Why don't you try walking across this motel room?"

I had no idea what he was trying to prove, so I started to walk toward the door.

I almost fell to the floor, but he caught me with his strong arms.

Whoa.

The fight with Caelius had sucked more juice out of me than I'd thought.

Aidan led me to the bed and forced me to sit down.

"Just give me an hour or two," I pleaded. "I'll be back to normal."

Tucking my hair behind my ears, Aidan smiled gently. "Rest, please? I'll stay in contact, and if I find him, I won't attack without you. But I'm going to try and find him alone, okay? Just like when you were in Paris."

I stood up abruptly, ignoring my dizziness. "I'm not letting you go alone. I'll heal as we travel."

Aidan slumped, defeated. "Shea, seriously? You're going to fight me on this?"

Seeing Aidan so scared for my well-being, I couldn't force him to take me along, but I had no intention of staying put. As soon as he left, I'd leave on my own.

I sighed, trying to act defeated. "Fine. But you have to

Dream-Walk with me every night."

I must have sold it, or Aidan just heard what he wanted to hear. He pulled me in for another hug and kissed the top of my head. Gotta admit, it felt good. Aidan had always been my safe place.

"Thank you," he said. "I promise I'll keep you posted, as long as you promise not to come running at the first sign of danger."

"I'm not a *super-being*. I don't move at lightning speed like all of you guys . . . do I?" I'd never tried it, but that didn't mean I couldn't do it.

Aidan shrugged. "Truthfully, I have no clue. Just please don't try it. You'll end up running into a brick wall or something."

"Thanks." I smacked him on the chest.

"Anytime." He smiled, glowing with an expression of implicit trust in me.

Well, *that* hurt to watch, knowing I was blatantly lying to him, but I smiled back all the same. "You'd better get a move on, mister."

I felt like such a horrible person.

Aidan nodded and hugged me one more time before he left.

It was good he left quickly because I was a terrible liar, and if Aidan had stayed any longer, he would have seen through me.

I waited a good hour before I figured he was long gone and I could start my own journey.

If I could just Dream-Walk with Lucian, he would be able to tell me where he was. Not that he *would*. I had no doubt that Lucian would try and hide the location, afraid I'd risk myself by coming to rescue him. But Lucian didn't have to *say* anything, because while Dream-Walking I could attempt to see his surroundings. Then I could maybe figure out where he was. A lot of ifs and maybes, but I had to try.

I closed my eyes and meditated until I fell asleep.

***

Dream-Walking was a strange thing. It was getting easier, but I'd grown so used to doing it with Aidan that I almost jumped inside his head automatically.

Luckily, I had enough control to stop myself and concentrate on Lucian.

Nothing.

As in, a big old block.

That was odd, because I'd Dream-Walked with Lucian enough that I could jump right in anytime I wanted. Either Caelius or Nefertiti was shutting me out.

Or, worse, Lucian was.

After hours of trying, I gave up.

In my desperation to find where Lucian was, I had a crazy idea. I tried brainstorming to think of anything else, but after a while, I sighed inwardly. It looked like crazy won out.

Ur-Nammu, here I come.

We had some serious Dream-Walking together in the past, so it wasn't hard to find him. He was awake, so I had more control over what we were going to see in our shared vision.

I picked somewhere familiar: the house with a porch swing that rested in the middle of a wheat field. It was where he'd taken me the first time we'd Dream-Walked. Somehow it seemed appropriate.

Ur-Nammu looked amused. "Shea Harper. I never expected to see you again, at least not in my subconscious."

"I'm stupid like that, I guess," I replied honestly. Then curiosity got the best of me. "How can you Dream-Walk and be awake?"

"I'm a fantastic multitasker," he answered with some bemusement. "And, as you should already know, vampires rarely sleep."

"You're in a good mood," I said. "I hear you're in Miami."

He closed his eyes in a moment of contentment. "To feel the sun on my face for the first time in thousands of years is truly breathtaking. I owe that to you, and I'm genuinely sorry for my part in how it happened."

"You did it for your daughter." I threw that out there to see his expression.

Ur-Nammu raised an eyebrow as if he knew where our conversation was heading. "Let me guess, Nefertiti has taken your Lucian."

I hated it when people could see right through me. "Well . . . yeah. Can you tell me where they are?"

"Why would I do that?"

Well, at least he didn't say no, which was better than I'd expected. I knew this was a long shot, but I couldn't think of any other way to find Lucian. "Because you want me to kill Caelius?" I hoped he'd go for it.

Ur-Nammu paused, eyeing me up and down. "You think you're capable?"

"Ask your daughter," I answered cryptically.

Wrong answer.

Ur-Nammu's hand wrapped around my throat. Even though I was sleeping, I still felt like I was being choked. "What did you do to my daughter?" he said, steel in his voice.

"Nothing!" I sputtered. "I hurt Caelius though. I'm assuming they're together!" I managed to say through garbled grunts.

"Oh." He let me go. "I apologize."

I rubbed my neck and felt oxygen rush back into my lungs. Dream-Walking was crazy. I wondered if I could really die in here. I didn't want to find out. I needed to tread more carefully. This guy was a master at the craft. I was just a noob.

"Jeez, I would never hurt your precious Nefertiti." I tried to hide the sarcasm in my tone, but I really felt like being a brat. "I can tell you hate Caelius as much as I do, and the only reason you helped him escape was because you wanted to live in the sunlight with your daughter. I get it. But wouldn't it be nice to not have to worry about Caelius ever again?"

Ur-Nammu paused for a moment, then gave a reflective sigh.

"I don't know where they are," he admitted.

"But you could—"

"I can do nothing. I'm still being disciplined for helping Lucian. Destroying the overzealous in Miami is my punishment. Contrary to popular belief, not all vampires like to torture and kill. Caelius will summon me when he feels I've learned my lesson. For him, that could be centuries." Ur-Nammu was definitely annoyed.

I felt bad for momentarily obliterating his good mood, but I couldn't leave without learning something useful. "All I want is Caelius dead and Lucian back with me. Can you help me or not?"

Ur-Nammu took a deep breath. "What if Lucian doesn't want to come back? Will you still help take down Caelius?"

So, Ur-Nammu didn't think Lucian would pick me over his daughter. It crushed my soul because I didn't think Lucian would either.

But I nodded. "Yes, of course. I'm made of Light or whatever. I think that means I was born to destroy Caelius."

He smiled sadly, and the sadness was meant for me, which made it worse. "I'm sorry, Shea Harper, I truly am, but Nefertiti will always be Lucian's true love. Yours was but a shadow of what they had."

I didn't argue. My defensive button wanted to snipe back at him, but what would I say? "Nuh-uh" or "You don't know!" Both sounded desperate and lame, even though desperate and lame was exactly how I felt. "Can you help me or what?"

Ur-Nammu nodded slowly. "I will send someone who can help. They will know where Caelius holds Nefertiti and Lucian."

Something about what he said struck me as odd. "What do you mean *holds* Nefertiti? Lucian's *their* prisoner."

His eyes were distant, even sadder than before. "Why do you think Lucian didn't know that female vampires exist?"

I hadn't thought about it. I was too wrapped up in Nefertiti cradling Lucian to care. "She hid from him? I don't know."

Ur-Nammu clenched his hands into fists as he said, "My beautiful daughter went from one master to another. Caelius kept her hidden. She's been his slave for over three thousand years. I knew that when Caelius was freed from his prison, he'd allow her to show herself. She'd still *belong* to Caelius, but at least she wouldn't have to hide anymore." Ur-Nammu stared me down,

54

his expression determined. "Once Caelius is dead, Nefertiti will be free. I will make this happen with or without your help."

"I'm helping," I replied immediately. I hated that I felt a pang of sympathy for Nefertiti, my competition. To be a slave for thousands of years, to be *Caelius's* slave . . . I shuddered. No one deserved that. No one.

Ur-Nammu nodded once. "Then we have a pact."

A pact? I didn't like the sound of that, but I'd do anything to find Lucian. "Agreed."

"I'll send her now," he said formally.

I woke up.

Her?

CHAPTER 4
LUCIAN

My eyes twitched. They were frozen open like a living corpse. Now I knew what it was like to be dead. All these years I'd felt hollow, empty, a reanimated shell. Shea had brought me back to the boy in Gutium. The boy, not the monster.

Now as my vacant eyes stared out, unable to blink, I knew that I'd never deserve her. Shea was my Eden, and I was nothing more than Adam tasting the apple's sweet nectar. It would have been better if Caelius had finished me off alongside Gracuri. I'd rather die than be used as bait.

My chest convulsed slightly. Drained as I was, the pain of his loss was unbearable. Now that I was in the same situation, I understood his foolishness completely, and his love. I would do anything to prevent Shea from coming to me. I would endure any torture if it meant her safety, just like he had.

I used all the power I had left in my weak senses to sever our dream connection. She wouldn't find me here.

Caelius moved from the corner of the room. How long had he been standing there? He laughed, casually walking over to my chains, where I was mounted to the wall like a prize elk.

He sat down by my feet. I jerked, but the chains were too tight. He ran his hands up my leg, then rested his head on my calf. "So you would still defy me, Lucian, even to your last drop of blood. How cliché and unreasonable. I find it enthralling nonetheless."

I forced myself to look down. Moving my eyes felt like dragging sand over glass. I tried to speak, to voice my hate. Nothing came out but a strange wheezing sound.

Caelius smiled, rubbing the side of his face on my jeans like a cat marking its territory. "What's that, my boy? I can barely hear you." Quicker than any movement I could register, he was standing and squeezing my mouth in fury, his lips inches from mine. It took a moment for my eyes to meet his. He waited.

I saw his distorted face. He'd been visibly thrashed; I could see the pink flesh covering his cheeks. If I'd had the energy, I would have smiled at him. I knew it was Shea who had given him that new face-lift.

He squeezed my cheeks harder. Different emotions clouded his eyes: obsession, lust, calculation. It was the last one that always frightened me. When his mind was contemplating his next step, the only real thing, the only promise, was of a future filled with agony. And Caelius *always* planned in advance. If he was planning now, then something had changed: a new calculation was being added.

Shea had changed the game.

He released my face and patted me on the cheek. My

emaciated skin hung from my bones. It twitched as he playfully tapped my jaw. I ignored the pain and watched through half-closed eyes as Caelius turned away and walked to the edge of the cell. He exited through a wooden door and left me alone.

I slowly took in my surroundings. I was in an underground cavern, and everything was wet.

Then I smelled it.

Blood.

Fresh and pumping.

Instinctually, my body jerked toward the smell, rattling the chains. I was on autopilot. My body was reacting without thought, without reason.

I tried to clear my head and regain control as Caelius returned, shoving a man and a woman into the cell. My fangs enlarged, and I snapped at the air like a rabid dog, saliva dripping from my mouth. Wherever Shea was, I was glad she couldn't see this.

Caelius stepped toward me. "Now there, Son. Don't hurt yourself any further. Let me bring them to you."

They were begging. The man was pleading for Caelius to spare his wife, to only take his life and let her live. The woman was doing the same, countering his plea with a heartfelt cry of her own for self-sacrifice. It amused Caelius at first, but then his expression shifted. His face soured from glee to disgust, then boredom. It was always that way when he thought he'd won.

"Come," he commanded, "step in front of my Lucian and offer up your necks." The man's eyes glazed over, and he marched toward my feral body, completely compelled. The woman hesitated.

Caelius stepped next to her and whispered into her ear. As

he was speaking, her face softened, then she stepped beside her husband, exposing her neck.

I yelled for them to run, but nothing came out, only puffs of air followed by maddened snapping. I tried to remember the mound of bodies and Gracuri, how I was more than my body, more than . . . this.

When they were inches from me, I smelled it. Not just blood, but a familiar scent. Did I know these people? My eyes met Caelius's in horror. Were these the lingering remainders of Gracuri's children? No. One was female, and they were still human.

Still, there was a familiar scent in the air that I couldn't place. Even as my body strained toward them, pulling savagely against the chains, within I surged against myself. I shifted that one small drop of blood floating in my bones to my vocal chords, reanimating them.

"Caelius, I'll do what you want. Just let these innocent people go."

He stepped casually beside them, straightening his all-white suit: Gracuri's suit. Not the one Gracuri had worn often, but my *favorite* suit, the one I loved seeing him in.

Gracuri had always looked like the morning, all covered in white, as if he were Helios himself riding his fiery chariot across the sky. It crushed my soul seeing Caelius flaunt it now, wearing it like a newly skinned mink coat.

The jacket should have been too big, but he'd already had it tailored. It still *smelled* like Gracuri though. Of course he wouldn't have it washed—that would take away its usefulness in reminding me of what he'd done, of what my disobedience had cost. I couldn't growl or fight. I just stared as the gleeful expression on Caelius's face returned.

My mouth pulled open, forced wide as my fangs grew longer, reaching for the woman's supple neck. I couldn't stop this. If this was even *real*. Everything was slow, indistinct, covered in a thick fog of conflicting impulses. My thoughts were everywhere, dissolving like mud across the water. But if this was happening, if I was going to eat two innocent humans while being ruled by uncontrollable instinct and not willpower, how could I look at Shea again? I was trying so hard to change. I had to be more than Caelius's pet. She deserved that much.

Caelius leaned closer, thrusting himself between the woman and me, whispering smugly, "Oh, are you still waiting for my answer? Of course I'll spare them . . . if they mean that much to you. I just thought you might be hungry. I'll tell you what, I'll let them stay the night with you and have a little Lucian sleepover. If they're alive in the morning, I'll honor my word and take them home. It's a simple deal, and I'm in the mood to make deals, seeing as I'm wearing apparel by Gracuri. Didn't you make a deal with him once as well? Wasn't that your cute little code when you turned him?"

He ran his thumb along the man's neck, his nail sinking in. The hairline cut bled instantly. Then he reached over and did the same to the woman. The smell of it was intoxicating. I shook my head, begging myself. *You're better than this, Lucian. Think of the cost. These people are important. You can feel it. They're innocent.*

Caelius slammed the rusted metal door. My eyes blackened just as my teeth savagely sunk into the woman's neck. Fear and terror etched into her blue eyes as I ripped through the meat of her throat.

***

Everything blurred. When my senses returned, I was inches away from Nefertiti. She held a rag and basin. She softly dragged the wet cotton over my face as I stared into her purple eyes. They'd been a strange color when she was alive: dark, almost black, but when the sun hit them you could see the violet.

"I always thought you were meant to be the ruler of our people, Nefertiti. Even your eyes were unique and beautiful. You were unlike anyone in our tribe." It was a strange thing to say. But my mind was lost: the starvation, the feeding. Besides, what would she care? This was just a hallucination.

I'd seen it happen before. I'd even caused it in Frank after he'd tried to drink Shea. Drain a vampire enough, and before their true death they'd see the faces of those they loved the most . . . those they'd killed.

She smiled. My insides warmed and melted the way they always had. Nefertiti wasn't a bad ambassador of death. She touched the cool rag to my forehead, wiping off blood and bits of meat. "In some cultures, purple is the color of royalty. It certainly was enough for the Pharaoh to single me out from the other Gutian women, to claim me as his own. And Caelius, well, that had more to do with you, Lucian, and less about *my* worth."

I looked deeper into her eyes. Now they seemed alight somehow, bright even in the darkness. "I would have killed the Pharaoh a million times over, had I been an immortal then. But I was just a boy when I died. And you were my everything."

61

She stopped cleaning my face and leaned in, bringing her lips close to mine. I closed my eyes, sensing only her fragrant smell.

She touched the engraved emerald necklace at my chest. It had been a gift to her when I was a boy. My memories were flooded with our shared moments. Our first kiss by the riverbanks: I'd been ten, and she'd been twelve. I'd thought about that kiss every night after. She'd had me then. My thoughts, my will, they were hers to do with as she wished.

She whispered, "I mourned for you in silence when you were being whipped outside my window. I never told you, but I was there when the Pharaoh was having you tortured . . . and I couldn't let you die, not my La-Narru. But that doesn't matter. I'm here with you now." Her voice was soft like gossamer. "Lucian . . ." It was rich like the aroma of rosemary. "Do you love her?"

I opened my eyes. Nefertiti's face was vulnerable. I'd never seen her look so troubled. She had always worn a mask of complete confidence, even in youth. I reached for her, but the shackles quickly reminded me where I was.

La-Narru.

That was a name I hadn't heard since we'd been children. It was the name my mother had called me. It was Caelius who'd given me a new name—Lucian—and with it, a new life.

My mouth fell open. How could I have forgotten? I hadn't been "Lucian" until his teeth had sunk into my young neck. My birthright, my very name had changed. *La-Narru.* It had meant something in my native tongue. It meant—

"Do you love her?" She leaned closer.

"Whom are you speaking of?" I pulled back. "Whom do I love?"

Nefertiti dipped the rag into the basin, then let the water pour down my face as she squeezed it over my tangled hair. "Shea Harper."

I looked at her, puzzled. "Shea is alive. And we are both dead, my sweet Nefari. You are no doubt preparing me to pass through the Nile with Anubis. Or is it to mount the Steed of Oknah in Gutium so it can carry my soul to the stars?"

I paused, holding Nefertiti's steady gaze with my own. "We both know I don't deserve either. I deserve Caelius. I deserve the black endlessness of his oblivion. But somehow you being the apparition of my harrowing tells me that my death may be a sweet one."

Her eyes softened further. "He really broke you this time. He forced me to watch, always in his shadow. The things I've seen him do to you, my only love. It pains my heart to see you so weak. I never should have—" She brought her thick, full lips close to mine. They smelled like honey, like they used to, and the taste . . . she hovered there, just out of reach.

Her violet eyes didn't blink. She was frozen like the sculptures I'd made of her likeness in Egypt. I'd molded them out of mud and straw, unworthy things that failed to mimic her perfection.

She moved closer. "My sweet La-Narru, I haven't heard you say Nefari since before I was a slave, before the Pharaoh made me Nefertiti. Do you still see me like that, like the girl by the riverbank in Gutium?"

I smiled, wanting to touch the soft curve of her back. "You have and always will be Nefari, a jewel among stones, my morning star."

She wet her lips and touched my cheek. "You are stronger

than your father ever imagined . . . stronger than I knew as a mortal woman. You are fearless now. The warrior you've become could have easily led us into battle centuries ago. And I would have stayed by your side. I would have ruled by your side. I would have been *yours*."

I pulled away—to see her incisors grow.

My head hit the wall I was chained to. Nefertiti leaned in closer. Before her lips could touch mine, one thought escaped into a single word. "Shea," I uttered.

Nefertiti jerked back, scowling.

"Why did you ask if I love her?" I demanded. "Why in death does that matter?"

She closed her eyes.

I waited in silence. I didn't know why I'd asked that. At the moment I couldn't remember what "Shea" meant. I just felt . . . felt that . . . that something wasn't right.

I was grasping, reaching, but every thought was scattered. Caelius had never brought me to the point of near extinction before. It was different when I'd been inside him, disappearing into nothingness. At that time, the ache and emptiness had burned a hole in me that no amount of sunlight could fill. But this? It was like when I was a child and had caught fever. I'd been close to death then, my mother mourning at my side.

"My mother . . . Anna-Steen." Her name caught in my throat.

I hadn't thought of her in so long. Now my thoughts drifted from beast, to man, to boyhood. I remembered the wildness of my mother's brown hair and the soil underneath her nails. She was a kind woman—too kind—and my father loved her with all the might of a raging lion.

They'd fallen in love when he and his people had raided her village. My mother had faced him, Onack the Great, with nothing more than a spinning needle in her hands. He'd often touch the scar down his left eye when he looked at her. If she caught him staring, they'd both smile, then he'd attack. They would roll to the floor, feigning brutalities like children, all the while laughing. It was how I'd known love existed in the world, that it was real, ageless, and infinite. They came from cultures that hated each other: it was in their blood. But love saw past that.

The shadow of the man that'd been left when she'd died next to me, both of us caught in the same fever, was how I'd learned what it was like to lose that love.

Then the wars had come. When my father stayed to fight, he'd begged me to leave, to live the life of a craftsman and a poet like my mother had wanted, but I'd refused. I would have rather died than leave Onack's side. But he pleaded that he wasn't strong enough to bear witness to the death of *all* that he loved, all that he had left worth fighting for.

I shook my head, remembering the tears in Onack's brown eyes. He'd been a large man, larger than the men they spit out like emaciated models now: like me. I never had the warrior's build of my father or Ur-Nammu. I had Anna-Steen's tall, slender frame, her gentle spirit, her teal eyes.

After her death, it'd been the color alone that'd prevented him from looking directly at me. Still, I shouldn't have let his tears affect my judgment—but he *never* cried. When they'd burned my mother's body, he hadn't shed a tear. He'd kept his grief trapped under layers of muscle and rage.

But on the night before battle, when I'd prepared to stand

beside him, Onack the Great's tears had tumbled out like an avalanche.

My lips parted. "How could I refuse my own father?" I gasped out the words, lost in my own conclusions. "To break his heart twice over by standing against the might of Egypt with hands that had held a paintbrush longer than a spear?"

Nefertiti's voice pulled me from the painful memory. She whispered quietly, "No one blames you, Lucian. You were being obedient, doing what your father asked, what we all asked. No one thought you a coward." Nefari's face was soft again, her eyes penetrating. My gaze followed the long black lines of makeup angled to a point on the corner of her eyelids. She looked like she had in Egypt, not Gutium.

She smiled. "Your expression, La-Narru. Your thoughts are drifting again. It's difficult to follow. I've rarely heard you reminisce about your parents."

I reached out and caught a piece of her black hair. I pulled the strands closer. They were soft and slipped through my fingertips like silk. "That's because it's too painful. Some things are better kept out of the mind . . . like you. I grieved over your loss for so long. Then I just filled that longing with sand—as I'd done with my mother's burned ashes after her funeral."

Her lips opened, and Nefertiti gazed at me like I was a helpless child. "When your father whipped you after your mother's death, that black soot covering your mouth . . . was her ashes?" She closed her eyes, and so did I. I could still hear the fury in his voice.

No one but Onack knew why my face had been covered in ash. My father had tied me to a post. The whip he'd wielded had torn the flesh from my back. I'd wept then. I'd screamed out into the sun, crying, not for him to stop, but from the pain of losing my mother.

The whole village had gathered. Ur-Nammu had tried to pull him back, but he was no match for Onack, a wild ox of a grieving man. He hadn't heard their pleas. It was only when Nefari had thrown her small body in front of my own—bracing for the whip, trying to protect me—that he'd paused.

I opened my eyes, pulling away from the memory and the pain of loss.

Nefertiti's eyes were full of compassion, her lips trembling as she spoke. "You know your father didn't mean to hurt you, La-Narru. Catching you choking on your mother's ashes must have blinded him, but he loved you." She grabbed the wet rag and let the cold water drip down my back, over the deep scars.

My gaze hardened. I felt the memory's sting as if the childhood wounds were still gaping open. "I know he loved me. But his lashings hurt more than any I received on your behalf in Egypt, Nefari. Because Onack was *right*. My mother died, and I lived. She was stronger than I was. *She* should have overcome the fever, not me."

She wrapped her arm around my neck and rested her head on my chest. "You have to know that it wasn't your fault."

I shook my head. Why lie, especially now that I was dead?

"You're wrong, Nefari; it *was* my fault. I was the one who wanted to see the marketplace. I didn't want to follow in my father's footsteps—I wanted to leave Gutium, to see the world past our village. If she'd never taken me, we wouldn't have gotten poisoned from the tea she purchased there. The tea *I* wanted. The tea I *begged* her to buy. It was the last time, before Shea, that I begged for anything. The last time I said '*please.*' My desires, my hunger, poisoned my own mother. She died because of me."

She fell silent, only shaking her head, concern flooding her features.

"I'm glad my father caught me. When Anna-Steen died and I ate her ashes, I'm glad he saw. I'm glad it infuriated him enough to beat me. I'm glad—"

She kissed my lips. Without a thought, without a word, I felt the rich, soft nectar of her touch. She pulled away slowly, her eyes burning into mine.

"Quiet now, La-Narru. Thinking of these things will keep you weak, and you have to regain your strength. Caelius has a plan for using you, but he could easily change his mind and decide to kill you, whether or not he's promised me your safety. You have to come back to me . . . you have to come back to your power, Lucian. You have to regain your senses."

I looked at her. She'd been the only one I'd loved after my mother's death, the only reminder that love could still exist in the world. I hadn't been able to stuff her ashes down my throat when I'd killed her; her father had taken her body. But I drank the sands of Egypt for years, hoping to dull the pain.

"I loved you, Nefari."

Her mouth opened, and for a moment she leaned closer, closing her eyes. Then she stopped. "You loved me, like you loved your father . . . your mother . . ."

I nodded, pulling against the chains, trying to touch her.

"Like you loved . . . Shea Harper."

"Yes."

Nefertiti stepped back, sighing. She let the rag in her hand fall into the basin. "So, it's true. You love her. It's not just boredom or infatuation."

I blinked, confused. "I'm simply reliving my life. This is the pathway before death. Mine is long because I've lived thousands of years. Some that I've killed relive their existence in a matter of moments. Are you the part of my mind that is fighting death? Why would I ask myself a question I already know the answer to?

"Of course I love Shea. I love her body and soul. With her I feel . . . alive. But it's so much more. I feel like I did when I used to watch my parents sneak kisses in the garden, that sense of wonder when I look into her eyes. Like I've known her in other lifetimes, in the depths of forever. If there is an eternity, or was, I will *always* know her. These forms we find each other in now are meaningless and will pass away, but our love will always pull us back together across time, across any distance. Like the ships of Gorthos, and Andromeda and her fated lover—"

"Enough!" Nefertiti cried. "You have said enough." Now her eyes were hard and bone-dry. "You are clearly delusional. I will continue to care for you until you regain your mind. But you should know that you're not dying, Lucian. I would never let Caelius or *anyone* take you from me. Not in Egypt. Not now."

Nefertiti's face looked like it had before battle—fierce and angry. "I'm the one who heard of the powerful man by the Nile. I'm the one who sent Caelius to find you after the Pharaoh decided to kill you. The bargain was for my life, my loyalty, and my secrecy.

"Caelius turned you because of *me*, La-Narru. After you were a vampire, he turned me in secret later that night. That was the

69

price *I* paid to save you: eternal enslavement. When you tried to turn me, you thought I'd died, but I only feigned death. I was already a vampire. Caelius made me live in hiding afterward."

I reeled in horror. What was she saying? What torment was this? That I was still alive, and she'd been *turned* by Caelius before he'd been imprisoned? Impossible! This was the madness before death.

Caelius sauntered through the door. "I'm sorry, dear, but that's all the time I will allow you today."

Nefertiti nodded and, without so much as a second look, left the room.

Caelius moved toward me, eyeing my beaten frame. Cupping my face in his palm, he tilted his head. "See how obedient she is? I trained her well. You just have to know someone's weakness . . . and squeeze." He grabbed a tuft of my hair and pulled my head back.

He raked his lips over my exposed neck. "You and her family are *her* weaknesses. My promise to keep you all safe, to keep you together, well, that's been enough for my girl to stay obediently at my side. Nefertiti's a good pet, unlike you."

I jerked at the chains, growling. I couldn't piece together their words. It didn't make sense.

Caelius let my head drop and then sighed. "What fun is teasing you when your brain is fevered like mush? If you continue down this spiral you'll have another true death, Lucian, one I can't bring you back from. Then what would I do? I'd be inconsolable.

"It *is* curious, though. I've often wondered what would happen if I drank you down to one drop, as I did today. I'm somewhat disappointed that it's left you in what smells like some

70

kind of human illness. Well then, let's get you mended so we can have our fun, my darling."

He snapped his fingers. As if they were mice following a flute, mindless humans scuttled in a line behind him until the entire cell was packed like canned meat.

"Dinnertime."

CHAPTER 5
SHEA

Whoever this *helper* was that Ur-Nammu was sending me, she was certainly taking her time getting here.

Her.

Another female vampire.

I was still reeling at the fact that Nefertiti was an old-as-dirt-vampire as well. It made me feel better to think of her as crone-ish. Catty of me, yet satisfying.

Maybe it was Nefertiti herself who was coming? I hoped not. I wasn't ready to face that particular demon just yet. Besides, Ur-Nammu had said Nefertiti was a prisoner and had been a slave for thousands of years.

I shuddered. Being in the room with Caelius for five minutes had been torturous, but century after century? I was surprised the girl wasn't batshit insane by now.

I needed to stay focused on rescuing Lucian. Even if he picked Nefertiti over me, I loved him regardless. I would never leave him to Caelius. Whether or not his feelings had changed, it didn't matter.

Ugh.

Of course it mattered.

I had to push those kinds of thoughts away. It hurt too much to think about him not loving me. Or worse: loving her more.

I stood up and stretched. My strength was coming back slowly but surely. I couldn't believe how much kicking Caelius's butt had drained me.

He was so powerful that every time I hurt him it took a chunk out of my energy. I hoped I'd given him reason to pause when thinking about confronting me again, but the guy was so full of himself he was probably just licking his wounds and planning his next attack.

I was going to need a lot more power if I wanted to seriously injure the guy, let alone kill him.

I sat in a dumpy hotel room that I'd paid for in cash. I was sure Aidan could find me by scent or some other angel detective skill, but I wasn't going to leave a paper trail for him or anyone else to follow. I'd watched my fair share of police procedural shows.

Speaking of, with nothing to do but wait, I decided to flip on the TV and catch an episode or two. There was always some kind of marathon running on cable. Nothing like a good detective drama to put perspective on my life. I used to think the stories were unimaginably horrifying, filled with serial killers and murderers, but now they looked like kittens and puppies playing compared to a second with Caelius.

If only people knew how much of these fictionalized movies

and shows were actually real. It was better that they didn't. No one would leave their house. But then again, maybe they shouldn't. Not if Lucian's father gained his full strength back. The world would be changed forever. It would become a nightmare.

Shaking the dark thoughts from my mind, I switched stations until I found a nice '80s movie I could use to pleasantly escape from reality. Nothing like fluorescent fashion and big bangs to make me feel warm and fuzzy inside. I wanted to find Lucian, but I knew whomever Ur-Nammu was sending would be my only hope.

My mind drifted with curiosity. Who was this girl coming to help me? A vampire to be sure, but Aidan and Lucian had told me that only *men* could be vampires. Now suddenly Nefertiti was one and, possibly, whoever was coming?

How many females were there, and how had they hidden from Lucian for thousands of years? You'd think with the amount of time he'd been on the planet, Lucian might have had some inkling that girl vampires existed. It didn't make much sense. Then again, not much in my life did these days.

I jumped when I heard a knock on the door. It wasn't loud, but I'd been so wrapped up in my thoughts that the sound jolted my psyche. My palms were sweating. I mentally prepared myself to make my blood liquid sunshine if things went south.

Taking a deep breath, I walked to the shabby motel door and cracked it open, peering through cautiously.

"Are you *her*?" I greeted her, sounding like an idiot, something I realized as soon as I'd said it.

"If you're asking if I'm the one Ur-Nammu sent, then yes. I'm *her*," the woman replied brusquely.

She looked my age, but dang—she was drop-dead gorgeous. Her skin was golden brown, and her large, almond-shaped eyes were a stunning gold to match. High, sculpted cheekbones made her face appear as if it had been carved in clay, and even her nose was perfect and straight.

I'd assumed all vampires were pale from lack of sun, but she had a permanent sun-kissed glow that took my breath away.

"Are you going to let me in?" she asked impatiently.

Oops. I'd been staring. A lot.

I opened the door all the way and waved her inside. "I'm Shea." I figured she knew that, but it was my clever way of trying to find out her name.

"I know that," she responded as she entered the room.

The more direct approach would have to do. "And you are?"

"Mekytaten." She gracefully sat on the wooden armchair in the corner.

A chill ran down my spine. I'd always been a little obsessed with the history of Nefertiti (now I knew why: stupid intuition!) so I knew all of her daughters' names. Mekytaten was her second oldest.

Man.

Nefertiti's daughter was as beautiful as she was.

I felt sick to my stomach. How could I compete with utter perfection? I was like the ugly kid-sister compared to this family tree. Why on earth would Lucian pick me when he could have Nefertiti? And it was a pretty good bet he knew all her daughters. He'd probably planned on rescuing them along with Nefertiti. When she'd died—or, more accurately, when he *thought* she'd died—Lucian's hopes and dreams had died with her.

The weird part of this was that history stated the Pharaoh Akhenaten had died *before* Nefertiti, but Lucian had said she'd still been Akhenaten's slave when she'd died. Of course, history also made it sound like the Pharaoh had loved Nefertiti with all his heart, and Lucian had claimed that wasn't true either.

It made me wonder how much of the past that I'd learned from history books was wrong. It reminded me of the telephone game, where you whisper a sentence in someone's ear and so on, until it gets back to you, and the original statement is unrecognizable. Too many half-truths and lies. People in power wanted to write their own story. What would a true recounting sound like? Probably nastier and a lot more dramatic.

"From the look on your face, I can see you know who I am." Mekytaten seemed impressed.

It was hard to imagine this girl was only a little younger than Lucian. She dressed like someone my age: striped crop, tight jeans, Chuck Taylors. I'd imagined she'd show up in robes and gold jewelry like the hieroglyphs depicted ancient Egyptians wearing. It was jarring to see her dressed as a normal teenager.

I decided I should stop gaping and actually speak. "I know a little bit of history. I admired your mother in school." I went with polite. No sense in pissing off She-Vamp.

"Admired. Past tense." She eyed me with judgment.

"It's not as if I knew she was alive . . . until today," I uttered defensively. "Where have you guys been hiding, anyway?" Might as well start with the obvious questions.

Mekytaten watched me carefully for a few moments, then smiled reluctantly. "Sorry, I'm being rude. I've been listening to my mother rage about you for the last few months. I guess it rubbed off on me."

She sounded like a teenager. It struck me as bizarre. Mekytaten was ancient. She should've been talking like Lucian, all formal and eloquent.

Mekytaten gave a short laugh. "I'm a good adapter. I have to fit in, and no offense to Lucian and his children, but their language habits don't exactly *blend*."

"Did you just read my mind?" I was mortified.

"Don't worry. I can only hear you when you direct your thoughts at me. A Vessel's brain naturally shuts out vampires, but I'm particularly good at diving into the subconscious," she explained. "As far as I know, I'm the only vampire who can do it."

Then what Mekytaten had originally said hit me. "Nefertiti was *raging* about *me*?" I didn't like the sound of that.

She sighed. "Look, my mother's been in love with Lucian her entire existence. He's never loved anyone before or after her. Let's just say, you were unexpected."

"Oh."

"My grandfather sent me here for a reason. I know where Lucian and my mother are being kept. But we can't go there . . . yet."

"Yet?" I could see she had something in mind.

"You're still weak from your fight with Caelius, right?"

I hated to admit it, but I felt like I was recovering from being hit by a car. "A little. But I could face him."

Mekytaten shook her head. "No. You couldn't. You were acting on instinct and anger before. I'm shocked you hurt him as badly as you did, but Caelius recovers fast, and you don't."

Bluntness.

I really hated that trait at the moment.

"I don't know how long it will take me to recover, and we need to rescue Lucian." I knew it sounded pathetic, but I didn't care. I couldn't stand the thought of Lucian being starved and tortured by Caelius. What kind of hell was he enduring right now? I didn't want him with his father for a second longer.

"You know almost nothing about your abilities," she stated boldly. When my face radiated defensiveness, she put a hand up to placate me. "Don't get me wrong, Adnachiel and Lucian have taught you how to use your powers, but that's just the tip of the iceberg."

Hearing her use colloquialisms was just wrong. I realized in that moment that I was a historical bigot. Aidan had an excuse because he'd been born at the same time I was, but she was so old. Ur-Nammu was all official sounding when he talked, and I was betting on the fact that Nefertiti was too. It bothered me that Mekytaten sounded like she belonged in my time. It almost felt unfair, like she didn't have the right to be a teenager, to be like me.

"Tip of the iceberg, huh?" I crossed my arms and mocked her. Man, I was being a brat, but I couldn't control myself. "You're a couple decades off in your colloquialisms." Not really. I had used that sucker quite a few times myself, but I wanted to take Mekytaten down a notch. She was just too damn pretty.

Her face fell slightly. "I didn't mean anything by it." She was embarrassed.

I made her embarrassed.

I was a jerk.

An a-hole.

A mean girl.

I sat on the bed across from Mekytaten and sighed deeply. "I'm sorry. I'm totally jealous of your mom," I confessed. "And you. And . . . that's it. I'm defensive and taking it out on you. I'm a dick." No sense in beating around the bush. I'd never been a rude or inconsiderate person.

Well, now that I thought about it, I had been just as mean to Lucian when I'd first met him. What was it about vampires that brought out the worst in me? Maybe it was our inherent Light versus Dark. I had to control my attitude, or I would alienate the only person who could help me find Lucian.

Mekytaten's face softened, and she appeared relieved. "Looking like a teenager, I try very hard to adjust myself as the years go by, but when you've been alive as long as I have, it's difficult to keep up with all the advances, especially the language. I didn't even have to learn English for a long time. My grandfather and Lucian don't have to do this as much. Lucian is older than me; though he looks like he's in his twenties, he was actually in his thirties when he was turned. My mother is a couple years older than him," Mekytaten shared.

She was giving me insight into Lucian and her mother. This only made it harder, though, because now Nefertiti was becoming a real person with a real life to me.

Mekytaten was the daughter of a Pharaoh. That was huge. That was *her* reality. She and her sisters had obviously been allowed to grow into teenagers before Nefertiti had turned them. I wanted to know all the details, all the secrets and lies, and how they had managed to stay hidden for this long.

But that wasn't what Mekytaten was here for.

And before I had rudely berated her, I was pretty sure she had been trying to help me with my powers. "You were saying before about tips of icebergs?"

Mekytaten smiled. "I'll get right to it this time. I can teach you how to heal yourself, to regenerate. I want you to be at full power when we rescue my mother and Lucian."

My eyes widened. "I can do that?"

"Oh yes. But I have to take you somewhere. Will you let me?" Mekytaten asked delicately. "It's very far from here."

I was a little leery of giving Nefertiti's daughter my full trust, but the idea of learning how to heal quickly was too tempting to be cautious. "Are we going to fly?"

"Only my mother and Lucian can do that, but if you let me carry you, I can run faster than a human eye can see." She stood up and waited for my answer.

I rose to my feet and smiled nervously. "Let's do it."

Having what looked like a seventeen-year-old girl pick me up baby-style felt a little on the odd side. But she was one of the strongest vampires on Earth, so I was pretty sure I weighed nothing to her. When Aidan carried me like this, it somehow felt all protective and sexy. With Mekytaten it was just awkward.

I shyly wrapped my arms around her neck. As fast as we were about to go, I didn't want to fly off her. She appeared oblivious to my discomfort, clearly focused on where she was about to take me.

"Mekytaten?" I asked.

"You can call me Meky. It's less formal."

This seemed to be a big deal to her, so I assumed it was an offer of friendship. I nodded and corrected myself. "Meky. Where

80

are we going?"

"Home," she answered, and then the world became a blur of motion and colors.

I'd already experienced this with Aidan and in a drugged-out stupor with Ur-Nammu, but this was different. She was faster. I could barely contain my glee as I felt the wind hit my face with enough g-force to make my skin pull back. It was exhilarating as the scenery streaked past us. I couldn't differentiate shapes, so I had no idea where we were. It wasn't until the ground beneath turned a deep blue in contrast to the bright sky that I knew we were running over the ocean. The ocean!

Home.

The word rang in my ears.

Egypt.

I knew it with certainty. Hadn't we just left there? Caelius's prison was just outside of Cairo, and I never wanted to go back. Lucian and I had enjoyed a particularly good time in that cave, but still, too many nightmares had been born from that prison. I didn't feel like drudging them up.

When Lucian and I had finally left the catacombs behind, he'd flown me to Paris. It had been a thrilling experience, soaring through the air in his arms. I'd been like Lois Lane with Superman, except my Clark Kent ate people. I decided I didn't want to think about it anymore.

As we ran faster, the blur around us turned to gold, and I knew we were in the desert. The pyramids were so large and shapely that they were the only blobs I could actually recognize.

Then we stopped.

It took me a second to gain my bearings. I didn't want to

puke all over Meky's Converse, so I took a few deep breaths and calmed my stomach.

When I finally felt well enough to be coherent, I surveyed my surroundings. We were in an abandoned Egyptian city. A few tourists were roaming through the ruins, so it wasn't a hidden place, but it wasn't exactly crowded either.

All that was left of the city were small two-foot walls twisting over the ground like a labyrinth. They must have been part of the foundation of buildings that no longer existed. There were a few platforms and smaller staircases and only one pillar in the distance. Its circumference was large, well over six feet in diameter. The top was broken off, but it was still over twenty feet tall.

"That pillar is the entrance to the temple. Come." Meky led the way.

To anyone watching, we looked like two college students visiting the ruins. If these people knew that this was Meky's home, where she had grown up, where she had lived, they'd probably want to pick her brain for details (after being completely terrified). Where had everything gone? What had been here back then? What had it been like?

When we reached the crumbling pillar, Meky traced her finger over a faded hieroglyph of the sun god, Aten. It glowed a deep yellow in response. I looked around, making sure no one saw us. Meky took my hand when the coast was clear, and everything went dark.

It took me a few seconds to realize we were underground. Meky lit four braziers placed around the chamber, then I could see more clearly.

The room was huge, larger than Caelius's prison. It was much nicer though. The walls, ceiling, and floor all had shiny gold inlay. Engravings covered almost every inch of space, all depicting the sun and what I could only assume was Aten.

It was stunning, an archeologist's dream. There were several doorways leading to more rooms. I felt like I'd stepped into a time machine and we were back in ancient Egypt. No movie or recreation had done it justice. This was the real deal, and I was honored to be experiencing it.

"My father built this place to hide us from Lucian, although Lucian thought Akhenaten had done it to hide from him after my mother had feigned death when he'd tried to turn her.

"As Pharaoh, Akhenaten made his people change their god to Aten, the sun god. It was the only way he could justify building the sun shields. He used ancient hieroglyphs from the Book of the Dead to hold the sunlight in the shields through the night. We couldn't leave, but Lucian couldn't get in either. My mother raised us here in these chambers, and in our seventeenth year she turned us," Meky explained.

"I thought your mother hated the Pharaoh, that he enslaved her." Lucian had made it very clear that Nefertiti was not in a happy marriage.

"She hated my father for a very long time. He'd kept her like a possession. He'd enslaved her and forced her to marry him. But after a time, and after all he did to keep her safe, to keep his daughters safe, she grew to love him.

"It cut her deeply when he died. Caelius forced us into his cave after that. He didn't want Lucian finding out about us." Meky's face turned cold and hard at the mention of Caelius. I knew how she felt. Then her eyes softened. "But my memories here are some of my favorites. We felt free here, my sisters and I, even if we weren't. I sometimes long for it more than I care to admit."

I felt so sorry for her, having been caged next to Caelius just so they wouldn't ruin some crazy surprise he had in store for Lucian.

"Eventually, Caelius let us up into the world in shifts, but in exchange we were sworn never to turn anyone. We were only to feed off the leftovers of Lucian's offspring so that he'd never suspect we existed." Meky shuddered at the memory.

"You had to eat vampire scraps your whole life?" My mind put her confession into perspective.

Meky shrugged. "At least we never had to do the killing ourselves. Now we drink from blood bags."

I nodded. Innocent vampires. It made me admire her in a way I hadn't expected.

Meky reached over and held both my hands so that we were facing each other. "Your power comes from the planet, from the elements. The sun is the strongest force of energy on Earth. Because of the ancient glyphs my father inscribed here, it is a wellspring of power. Because you are made of Light itself, you are the only one who can *feed* from it."

"Did any of the other Vessels know about this place?" I asked.

"No. Lucian would force Adnachiel to kill the Vessels before there was a chance to bring them here. We wanted to, you know. We wanted to make the Vessel strong and possibly destroy Caelius for good, but Lucian was too hell-bent on revenge against Adnachiel for us to try. And we had to hide our presence from Lucian, acting in the shadows." She smiled. "We were lucky this time. The Vessel ended up being too beautiful for Lucian to resist."

That was sweet, but I hated compliments. I had no idea how to respond, especially since I felt like a troll next to her. My face burned with embarrassment and I didn't speak, Meky let out a small laugh. "And humble too. Who would have thought?" She took my hands and placed them on a small altar made entirely of gold.

It was three feet high and about a foot wide, etched with symbols and words I couldn't understand, but I heard it humming. It was singing to me. It was a part of *me*. My soul was perfectly in tune with whatever power this altar held.

Meky pulled away in sharp pain, but her smile broadened. "Vampires may be able to walk in the sun now, but true Light is still poison to us." She nodded to the altar. "Feed, Shea Harper, and become the death of Caelius."

CHAPTER 6
LUCIAN

I stared at the cold, hard stone beneath my feet. Weak. That was my problem. No matter how much power I accumulated, no matter what I'd done or survived, I was still weak.

I didn't want to look up. I kept my gaze on a crooked stone. There was moss growing in its crack. I made my irises retract. I could see the moss like I was looking at it through a microscope. All of its pores, the way it swayed from a pencil-thin breeze that whispered through the cavern.

It was alive.

Alive, and more worthy to stay that way than I was.

I tried not to breathe. Breathing to a vampire was like drinking herbal tea. The air itself was constantly filled with an ambrosia, and when it circulated through my lungs it felt . . .

I sighed.

I couldn't.

I couldn't justify the pleasures of my species. Not after this.

I didn't have to look up. I could still hear their screams bouncing around in my memory as I'd fed. Now that the fog had lifted and my mind was fully conscious, I was powerful. Externally. My body surged with pleasure. And I hated it.

Caelius had won. He'd always win. If I was damaged enough, my instincts took over. The instincts of a starved *beast* with no loyalty.

How could Shea look at me again with those soft hazel eyes? She deserved better. She deserved Adnachiel.

"Bravo." Caelius started clapping as he leaned against the corner of the room.

When the fever in my brain had cleared three days ago, I'd known he was there . . . watching. He'd sent Nefertiti in to clean out the mess, but I hadn't let my gaze fall on Nefari or Caelius. Just this stone and tiny speck of moss.

I heard his ominous steps as he moved toward me. "Are you still moping? I've been reminding you, like a good father, of who you really *are*, haven't I? And now your own thoughts repeat my sentiments, don't they? Surely now you realize how much better you are than all of them! The Vessel is unworthy of the magnificent animal that you are! She's nothing more than a light bulb trapped in cow hide."

Caelius moved his hand through my hair. He squeezed the blood from one of my locks into his mouth. I cringed as he smiled. Then, with his thumb, he dragged a long line of red down the side of my cheek and over my bottom lip. As he pulled me in, he kissed me hard.

I didn't blink. I didn't move. I just focused on that stone. Caelius, angered by my impassivity, shoved my back against the wall. It cracked from impact. The chains binding me rattled as he kissed me again, pressing his white Gracuri suit against my hardened frame. He laughed as he licked the side of my neck. I prepared myself.

He'd been doing this for three days.

He'd fatten me up, then drain me. Over and over he'd plump me, then suck me down. In the caves he'd ravaged my body. The shadow had been able to leak from his cage and do what it wanted. But it hadn't been able to do this. It hadn't been able to *feed*.

Caelius sank his teeth in deep, moaning in ecstasy as he ran his hand down my lower back. He pulled up for a moment, turning my head to meet his gaze. My face moved, but my eyes were on the moss. "Of all the galaxies I've devoured, all of the worlds I've destroyed, I must say, my son"—he ignored my expressionless eyes—"you are the most delicious creation I have ever tasted. I wonder if it's the *me* in you that makes your blood so irresistible? No. I've tasted others who carry my blood. Even Nefertiti doesn't taste this sweet."

A low rumble left my chest, and finally I looked at him. My eyes burned into the auburn of his. He smiled wider. "Oh, there you are, *boy*. I wondered how long it would take for you to come out and play. This will be so much more enthralling if you're battling me throughout. The first ten times I fed and bled this weakened body of yours you were still recovering. You were so unsure of yourself, like a puppy.

"But now, now I see that old twinkle in your eyes, that rare spark that defines you, my favorite pet." He wrapped his arms around my waist and hugged me tight, then sank his teeth in and tore, ripping a gash with his incisors from my neck to my chin. With a sigh of satisfaction, Caelius pulled back as the red gushed over and drenched my torso.

"Now that you're with me, Lucian, we can finally have some *real* moments together." He reached down and grabbed my thigh, sinking his teeth into the thick muscle.

"You see, darling," he said between slurping gulps, "these humans I've been feeding you were just a test, a theory I developed after your little harlot Shea bounced me on her lap in the desert." Satiated for a moment, Caelius stood and nibbled on my ear.

He crudely wiped his mouth on his lapel and smiled. "You have her to thank, really. If I drink you down to one drop, you live . . . but your willpower is *gone*. Granted, your survival skills are already adapting." He traced my eyebrow with his thumb, his eyes filling with twisted fatherly pride.

Then he leaned in closer, speaking with intimate passion. "But it will take you a few hundred years to master *not* feeding when *I'm* the one who has drained you." Caelius pressed his hips against mine. When he drew back, bitterness masked his features. "While you were practicing with that *whore* in France, teaching her how to use her powers against me, you should have been preparing *yourself*."

I bit my tongue. I knew this game; he was provoking me. The more I fought, the more thrilling it was for him, and the more he'd want to raise the stakes. I shouldn't have made eye contact. But imagining him drinking Nefertiti and knowing about me and Shea in Paris . . . I had to do something.

Caelius licked my bottom lip and laughed. "Are you surprised? Of course I knew about Paris! I only used that mule Gracuri to draw you out so we could have some alone time. I missed you, darling. Speaking of that unworthy meat sack, that's our next little step in this process: your undeserving children."

I winced. Of course. Watching me feed off of my sons—my direct descendants, the three Gracuri had saved—would give Caelius the most power *and* the most pleasure.

Caelius grabbed my throat, letting his thumbnail push into my open gash. Eyes shifting, lighting like red flames, he brought his face close to mine and examined my expression. Then he breathed in deeply, enjoying the scent of my torment.

He kissed my eyes, whispering in a warm tone that was not without its own warped sincerity, "You see, beloved, I am so much stronger when feeding off of *your* blood. More so than from sucking on your sloppy Second-Borns. You are—because you are directly from me, of course—like a fine distillery."

My stomach lurched. I needed to take away anything he could use. I tried to empty myself of all emotion.

Caelius draped his arm around my shoulder and picked at my back, cutting a scar open as his temperament darkened. "I'll feed you the best cuts of meat, Lucian. The cuts *you've* chosen all these years, hand selected. And despite your *deep* affection for them, once I drink you down, you'll devour them willingly."

Then he buried his face in my chest and drank. My blood splattered across the walls as he sank his hands into my torso and fed with abandon.

He laughed, drunk on the sensation, then stopped suddenly, looking at his suit. "I'll need this cleaned again. What do you think, my love? I'll suck the delicious fermented power of your sons from your own delectable hide. Your father *needs* you, and now you can finally be of service." He grabbed the back of my neck and pulled my hair taut as he sank his teeth into my mouth. He lingered, tasting my lips before vanishing into the darkness.

I felt it; his power was radiating. If there was a God, I prayed Shea was out there somewhere practicing with Aidan, growing stronger. And I prayed that she'd never find me.

Because I needed to die, to let my body give in to death. Once I did what Caelius wanted, then, armed with the power of my Second-Borns, there would be no stopping him. It was too dangerous. I couldn't risk continuing and have him hurt Shea. But when I was maddened, I couldn't think. If I could just be conscious for a moment, one moment, I could push that last drop of blood that he would leave in me out of my bones and finally die a true death. But instincts always took over and kept it trapped inside.

A hand moved through my hair. I refocused my gaze on the mossy stone, preparing for the withdrawal. Waiting for him.

Soft fingers touched my neck, but I refused to make eye contact. I needed to focus, to be better than this. When I'd fed from Gracuri, his mind and soul had been *mine*. Now I would always carry that guilt. Even before he'd died, Gracuri hadn't fully shaken free from the influence of my feedings. It was all I could do, after every time Caelius fed, to keep myself sane and detached from his influence, to keep alive that free "wild spark" that he loved so much. But my body, everything inside, wanted to serve Caelius wholly and completely.

While at his mercy in the cave, I'd always found a way to master his torments and pull myself back together. This time was different. My mind was staying in a fog for so long . . . too long. Now I was conscious enough to see what I'd done during my blood-starved crazes that Caelius had engineered. I *knew* the countless lives I had taken.

"Lucian . . . La-Narru . . ."

I shifted my eyes from the stone and looked down into Nefertiti's purple gaze. And finally I breathed. I could be human for a moment. "Nefari . . ." I shook my head, at a loss for words. What could I say to her? The last time we'd spoken I'd thought she was an apparition. Now I'd had time to think about everything she'd said and done.

"Nefari . . ."

She placed a hand over my lips. "Don't speak. Let me mend you." She turned to the side, offering her neck.

I jerked back in disgust. "I will *never* feed off of you, Nefertiti! I'm not like Caelius!"

She paused, staring into my hardened gaze. "I know." Then she turned her neck to me again, adding softly, "But you need your strength, and this is the way of our kind."

"Caelius is not our *kind*. We are and will always be Gutian. And I will not feed on your blood like some animal. Our people deserve more respect than that. Other than your father, Nefari, we are the last of our race—"

"Enough," she commanded with the authority of the Great Royal Wife she once had been. Nefertiti waved her hand in front of my face, then sank her teeth into her wrist.

I pushed away, but she held my throat in place and poured her blood into my neck and chest. I healed in those places instantly. Dipping her fingers into her blood, she touched all the bite marks and gouges covering my back and thighs. And, when she was finished, she licked her wrist, closing the wound.

I didn't know what to say.

"I'm sorry," I mumbled. It wasn't enough, but seeing Nefari like this was destroying me. "You gave your life to Caelius . . . you let him turn you . . . in order to save me?"

She nodded.

I leaned closer. "When I was threatened by the Pharaoh, you sought Caelius out. In exchange, he gave me life. If only I hadn't been so careless. It was my fault the Pharaoh found out about us. I should never have come to Egypt. You would have lived a long, normal, *human* life by his side. A slave to the Pharaoh, maybe. Imprisoned in the comfort of a glorious palace, surely. But not *this* hell with Caelius, and for so long . . ."

Nefertiti rested her hand on my chest, her touch gentle as always, but her eyes were somewhat calloused. "I'm glad you are no longer feverish, Lucian. Caelius did not empty you this time for a reason. He wants you *conscious* when he brings one of your Second-Borns here."

She ignored the expression of horror that crossed my face to explain in very clear detail what was in store. "Caelius wants you to look at your son's terrified face—to have that as the *last* image of your child—just before Caelius empties you, just before your will breaks and *you* devour your child."

And then, because she'd been a queen used to the burden of decision, Nefertiti said in clipped, stark sentences, "We have a short amount of time. He's hunting one of your sons now. You only have three children left besides my father, but they're all well hidden. I'm sorry about Gracuri."

Sorry?

I didn't understand. She had nothing to be sorry for. Gracuri had been found by Caelius. That was not her fault. None of *this* was her fault. I could only imagine what manipulations Caelius had used to keep Nefertiti hidden from me, to keep her by his side.

She looked away. "Caelius was close to finding all of them. I met with Gracuri and told him where to hide the others. He hid them well. He should have stayed hidden himself, but *I* drew him out."

I leaned back, letting her hand slip off of my chest. "Why?"

Her gaze fixed on mine. "I couldn't reach you. I tried, but you being with the Light blocked your mind from me. I asked Gracuri to find you. Because he is your blood, he only needed to call out. He would have told you that I was alive and of my plan to stop Caelius. It would have been so much simpler that way. But . . ."

Nefertiti looked through me, no doubt rethinking her plan, and seeing its flaws. She was a more brilliant strategist than her father, Ur-Nammu, ever could be, but she was still no match for Caelius. "He found us. I'm not sure how. I was careful. I'm always cautious."

I nodded. I knew all too well of how careful she could be. It had been *my* mistake in Egypt, not hers, that had led to my death.

She furrowed her brow. "I had no choice but to act as if I had hunted Gracuri myself, to present him as a gift. Caelius was easily convinced, clouded by his lust for that particular vampire. I know Gracuri meant something to you, Lucian. For that, I am sorry Gracuri's life was lost."

She paused, and in that pause I waited, looking over her features. They looked the same, frozen like the day I thought my kiss had killed her. But inside she had changed.

"I'm sure you've done a great deal of things to survive under his embrace," I said, understanding all too well. "I don't blame you for anything you've done or will do."

I knew it was my fault Gracuri had died. If I hadn't cared about him so deeply, Caelius wouldn't have singled him out. If it hadn't been his blood in my veins when I'd fought Caelius in the cavern . . .

My mind ached with remorse. "Don't carry that burden, Nefari. It's mine alone."

Her mouth fell open, but she closed it quickly. "Are you still that Gutian poet, that boy, all these years later, La-Narru? Can you find no reason to *hate* me?"

I pulled against the chains and reached for her, the edges cutting my wrists deeper. Placing her hands over her heart, she fell into my chest like she used to when we would meet in secret by the Nile. I'd be covered in mud and straw from working with the other slaves. The Great Royal Wife Nefertiti had worn white and been adorned in jewels.

She'd let the grit of my body fall on her dress. She never cared. Nefari would bathe afterward to hide the mess from the Pharaoh, but when she was with me, she'd been more than happy to be covered in filth. As long as we were together.

I breathed in the scent at the nape of her neck. I'd done that a million times when we were alive. I wasn't smelling her as a vampire, I was smelling her like a young man, remembering a time when I'd fallen so deeply in love that I'd been blinded to the world around me.

I sighed. "I could never hate you, Nefari."

She pulled back, her hands still cupped to her breast. "I hated *you.*"

I shook my head knowingly. She was as ancient as I was. She'd had time enough to think about all she had done and to grow in bitterness, to become something unrecognizable.

"I hated that I'd made that deal with Caelius because of my love for you. That one decision sentenced me to unimaginable torment. I was young, and I couldn't let you die."

She closed her eyes, probably reliving the moment of her turning like it was a fresh wound still open. "I'd just had my last child, Setepenre. She was so beautiful. A mother isn't supposed to pick favorites, but I know now as I did then: she is special.

"When I stared into her eyes, so full of life, as you were being whipped mercilessly outside my window, the thought that she would never see you—you had met all the other girls in secret, but she would never know your face—was more than I could bear at the time."

Nefertiti grabbed her waist, touching a long scar she'd received from giving birth, a scar that would never heal no matter how much blood she covered it with.

She pushed on the lesion and winced, rage covering her pristine features as it had on the eve before battle. "After Setepenre, I knew Akhenaten would kill you. You should have never made those clay sculptures of my image. And so many . . ."

I closed my eyes, trying and failing to drive out the pain of that time, the carelessness of my mistake. I hadn't been a warrior then. I had been a fool, and my love dangerous.

Nefertiti rested her soft frame against my wounded, chained body. Her lips pressed on my chest as she spoke, her voice low. "I heard whispers of a power greater than Akhenaten. 'Caelius,' they whispered, and I listened.

"When I found him, I made a deal for your salvation. I still had to watch as the Pharaoh had you tortured to the point of death. But Caelius turned you in time, changing your death into our everlasting perversion of life. Then he came for me later that night; that was our agreement. I did not resist him as he feasted on my blood.

"He said then that if I revealed myself to you before his plan came to fruition—revealed what I'd done, what I'd become— that he would kill us both. That had not been part of the agreement we had made, but, as you well know, once Caelius has you, he dictates his own terms. And then, later, he found many better ways to keep me in my place, to keep me shackled in the shadows away from your arms. But by then I had long realized my mistake. I knew it the first night I awoke as a vampire. I doomed our existence."

I leaned toward her. I used my chin to cup her neck, pulling her closer to my chest. "Nefari, you couldn't have known what he was. We came from a land of gods, a land that was ravaged without any word from those gods. And in Egypt there were new gods, and you were kept like a trophy of our failed beliefs by the Pharaoh."

An ache filled my chest. Now with the knowledge of Light and Darkness, of angels and vampires, I realized our naivety. We'd been so human then, so blind. "We'd learned through the slaughter of our kind to stop believing in anything but the love for our people, for one another. You couldn't have guessed, Nefari. You wouldn't have believed what Caelius was, what power and degradation he was capable of, even if he had told you."

I felt her lips curve as she whispered, "He did." They were soft as they moved upward on my neck. She exhaled for the first time since I'd seen her. One breath. And that was all, as if she'd been holding it for thousands of years. "I didn't believe him."

"I understand."

"Of course"—her voice turned flat—"you *would* understand." I knew her. Nefari's masked tone couldn't hide the storm raging inside. She'd always been more Gutian than I was, more passionate than the deep wells that boiled inside of me. Having become the Great Royal Wife in Egypt, she was better at concealing that passion, but it was there.

As Nefertiti pulled back, I opened my eyes. We looked at each other carefully for a moment before she spoke again, still holding tight the reins on her emotions.

"Eventually I stopped blaming you. Watching you devour the sands of Egypt in grief after you thought I was dead, it was all I could do to stay sane." Nefertiti paused, stepping farther back before she continued. "It was me, Lucian. I was the one who sealed us all to this fate. Who knows the people Caelius would have chosen as his Adam and Eve had I not turned his gaze on you. It was *my* doing. I alone am to blame for all you've suffered."

Her tone darkened, and so did her eyes, but I wasn't afraid. I knew she was hardening herself, deadening, preparing for the fury of my response. Nefertiti had waited thousands of years to have this conversation. She must have imagined a million ways that it could play out, all of which ended in my hate.

I looked at her powerful features, and all I saw was the little girl I'd grown up with. "We may have lost some of our beliefs in the war, Nefari, but the code our fathers created, that still burns. It's still alive in our Gutian bones. Those were our first words, the first thing taught to both of us. After all this time, I know you, and I know that you still believe it. I'll say this once, Nefertiti. I will *never* blame you. You thought you were fighting like our people had for the ones they loved. You thought the deal with Caelius would save my life. You risked everything—"

"For the one I love. And now he loves the Light. He loves Shea Harper."

I paused, stunned by her response.

"Nefari, I . . . I do love her."

She jerked back, out of the reach of my extended fingertips. I closed my eyes in frustration. I couldn't make it right. I didn't know how. To me, Nefari had been dead for three millennia. All I'd kept was her memory and the necklace I'd made for her as a child. I had searched for that necklace for *years* in the ashes of Pompeii. Before that I had always worn it. It was a constant reminder of her loss, of the only woman I'd ever loved. I felt it weigh heavily on my neck now.

But I had fallen for Shea, body and soul.

I needed time to process all that had happened. But it was impossible. With Caelius feeding off of me over and over like some fattened pig, I didn't know how I felt. I was lucky that I was strong enough to put my mind back together at all.

When I opened my eyes, she was staring. I looked closer. "What is it you're not telling me?"

She tilted her head curiously.

I shifted. She had a tell. I doubted even Caelius knew what it was. It was subtle. But I had watched her grow up. I'd watched the tell go from conscious to subconscious. When we'd been children, the gesture was large. But now her cheek barely moved when she bit the inside of it.

"What is it, Nefari?"

She scanned my body, looking for more gashes.

My voice hardened, and I stood tall. "I'm strong enough. Whatever you're going to say, do it now."

She nodded. "You're right. Who knows how long Caelius will be gone. Time is important. I'll only ask you this one last time. Think about your answer, La-Narru. Do you really love her?"

I would have nodded, but she deserved to hear it. "I loved you, Nefertiti. I will always love you. But you *died*. I mourned. You were buried with my heart in the sands of Egypt. I never thought I would find love again. And it's been thousands of years."

I paused. I didn't expect her to understand. To her I'd been alive all this time, just out of reach.

I breathed in deeply, letting her scent rest in my lungs, fully aware that after she heard my answer, I might never see her again. "Yes, Nefari. I love her. Shea found me when I was covered in darkness. She brought me back to who I'd been before Caelius, back to myself, to that Gutian boy who wanted life to be beautiful. She's a part of me now. I'm sorry. I'm sorry—"

"Of course." Nefertiti nodded, an impenetrable mask slowly covering her soft features. "I had to be sure. You said this before, but you were taken with fever then. I've had days to think about your response as I've watched Caelius toy with you. I watched him devour your flesh and strip you of your dignity. Even though what he's doing now is new, it reminds me of what he did to you in the caves."

"You . . . ?"

"Yes. I was there." Nefertiti's mask was almost in place, which made her pained words all the harder to bear. "No, Caelius never subjected me or my family to your unfathomable tortures. My punishment was *watching*. And I will *always* love you, La-Narru. But I understand. What you've suffered . . ."

Her hand reached up to cover her mouth in a sort of twisted horror, her eyes moving rapidly, no doubt analyzing the severity of my torment. When her hand fell away, she hardened again, certain of her response.

"You deserve better. You deserve to be loved, but also to be *protected*. Whether it's by me or Shea. And I have been working on a way to protect you. To protect us all.

"When you were fighting Caelius in the cave, I knew you couldn't kill him. If I hadn't stepped in, he would have killed all that I loved and made me watch. You don't know how hard it is to pretend to love Caelius when I truly despise that creature. I pulled him from the cell. It was a risk, but I knew the method I'd been working on could kill him. But I'll let her explain."

Decision made, she walked quickly across the room and opened a small side door. The sound raked my ears as the bottom edge of the wood dragged along the stone. My senses were heightened by Nefertiti's blood. It would make Caelius draining me that much more painful. It was agony, being juiced up on humans. I could feel every cell. Every twisted torment he concocted was done on newborn skin. And now with the power of my Second-Borns, it would be much worse. I'd go mad.

"Come in, Helena."

A slender woman entered. She eyed me in the darkness, then spoke assertively. "Why is he still chained? Is it as I've suspected? Are they angel bones?"

Nefertiti shuffled Helena closer, her voice a whisper. "If Caelius comes back before we have a chance, it will look like we're tending to his wounds. If his chains are removed, it will look like we're freeing him. We remove them at the last possible moment . . . if we even can."

Helena nodded as Nefertiti pushed her in front of me.

I stared in awe at her features. My brain still couldn't fathom the possibility, but she was here. Helena, the woman I'd befriended instead of fed on, the woman I would have turned into a vampire if my bite wouldn't have killed her. The child from Lorreto Chapel, the botanist from . . . a hundred years ago?

I stood dumbstruck. I spoke aloud, though it was more to myself. "How is this possible? You were killed in a train crash. You were pronounced dead. They never found the body."

Helena smirked and set her hand on her hip. It was an awkward gesture, but I remembered it. It was awkward because of her boyish physicality. She didn't look boyish—she was cute in a sweet sort of way—but her mannerisms had all the markings of a tomboy. She'd been raised with men. Six older brothers, if I remembered correctly.

Then Helena patted my shoulder, and her smirk widened until I saw . . . fangs.

And she saw my reaction.

"Nefertiti turned me," she explained, the scientist still strong in her personality. "Vampire genealogy is interesting. Males can turn males, and females can turn females, but you can't cross the wires."

Nefertiti stepped beside her. She wore a slight smile, as if I would be pleased. "I've watched you all these years, Lucian. When you took an interest in Helena, I did as well. I understood your fascination. She was brilliant for a human. I imagined what she could do with more time and a higher-functioning body."

I scowled. "I thought you said you'd learned over the years, Nefertiti? What was it you learned? Oh, yes, that this gift of life you gave me is a curse. I turned seven others, but I was twisted and wrong. Now I feel the regret of those decisions—"

Nefertiti waved dismissively, stopping my rambling. It was an authoritative gesture she'd picked up in Egypt. I hadn't liked it when she'd done it then, and I didn't like it now.

"It's not what you think, Lucian. Caelius forbade me from turning anyone because he didn't want you to know I was alive. He knew that you could trace any vampire that I'd turned back to me. It was too great a risk. And he so enjoyed your agony over my death and the idea of our perfect reunion."

Helena kept patting my shoulder as she sucked her bottom lip. She'd never been very comfortable talking about emotions. Science was the realm of comfort to which she belonged.

Nefertiti ignored Helena's awkwardness and continued. "When you befriended Helena, I studied her. I planned. I knew that she could help me find a cure for our condition or a way to fight Caelius, and your interest was the angle I needed. I talked about your infatuation with her, embellishing to Caelius. He sent scouts, and they watched you dance and laugh by her side, but you never fed. She wasn't like the dead humans you'd left in your wake at that time. You actually liked her as a person. That was rare for you."

I broke eye contact. At the time I'd met Helena, I'd been feeding just for the sake of bathing my hands in blood, anything to numb the boredom and pain of being what I was. And then . . . Helena. There'd been no immediate chemistry, and of course I'd tried to kill her, but she'd outsmarted me. *That* hadn't happened before. After, I'd realized who she was: the orphan from Lorreto, the one I had cared for when she'd been just a child.

Helena shifted nervously, then jabbed me on the shoulder. "How about that, Lucian? A botanist vampire. The only one of my kind. Caelius was fascinated by me for a while because of his obsession with you. But he grew bored. Nefertiti was able to convince him to let her keep me as a pet. His words, not mine."

I nodded. I was happy to see Helena, but not as a vampire. By now I was sure she knew that it would have been better had she died on that train.

Helena slipped her finger over my wrist, touching the bone exposed from pushing against the chains. She rubbed my blood between her fingertips like examining a lab sample. "It's just as I thought, Nefertiti. We won't be able to get him out easily. A smart move on Caelius's part. Lucian can't escape when he's all hopped-up on the blood of his own children."

She wrinkled her brow, looking closely at my bloodied wrists, then at my ankles, her irises widening. "Your wounds aren't healing at these places because Caelius made these chains from Adnachiel's brother's bones, the one he tortured and devoured in the caves. Caelius has stored them somehow. Maybe . . . inside of himself?" Helena's face sparkled. "Like an undigested femur in his stomach? Amazing creature, that Caelius."

Nefertiti's and my gaze fell on her with disdain for what sounded like adoration.

Helena rested her hand on her hip again, slightly embarrassed. "Not like that, I mean, not 'amazing' himself, but from an objective point of view, Caelius would be worth dissecting in a lab."

Even through my own pain, I had to grin. "That, Helena, I'd love to see."

Her eyes met mine in eager agreement. We had a similar sense of humor.

But it wasn't that much of a joke to Helena, who rattled on. "Of course it can be done; I've been working on something along those lines for a couple decades now. But first there's the matter of the parents. I've kept their bodies, but what do *you* want to do?"

My puzzled expression must've confused her. She looked at Nefertiti. "You haven't told him yet? What have you been doing in here this whole time? Caelius just left, and we need to set this plan in motion immediately, but Lucian deserves to know. And I deserve to get that stink out of my lab."

Nefertiti waved her hand, and Helena stopped talking. I assumed that over the course of a hundred years she'd learned that motion meant not to cross her. Maybe Helena really had become her pet, as Caelius believed.

"No, I haven't told him," Nefertiti explained slowly. "I wasn't sure if it was necessary. But seeing that Lucian actually *loves* this Shea, then yes, he deserves to know and to decide for himself."

Nefari paused, then faced me. "You killed Shea Harper's parents. The first night you were here, Caelius left them in your cell. You drained them. I was able to drag away the bodies. Helena has been keeping them preserved. The choice is yours."

My body collapsed. The chains holding the shredded meat at my wrists were the only things keeping me from hitting the floor. I could feel bone grate against the steel. It was painful, and I was glad for it. I closed my eyes. There was no going back from this. Shea would *never* forgive me.

That first night of Caelius's torture, caught in the blood fever he'd overwhelmed me with, I'd thought the people he brought in were familiar. I'd thought it was Gracuri's suit, but Shea's smell must have been on them, *in* them. How could I not have known?

Nefertiti's voice was low, soft. "Caelius chose them specifically your first night here. It wasn't your fault."

"Don't placate me, Nefari," I snapped.

She fell silent.

I hung there on my chains, unwilling to rise. Her words didn't matter; there was no point to anything I did now. When I'd seen Nefari again, there'd been hope. A small part of me, a part that was more Aidan than Lucian, had thought that I might survive Caelius's tortures, that I could still help Shea fight him. I'd hoped she would understand all that I'd done, that I'd not yet adapted to being leached by Caelius.

That I wasn't a monster.

But this . . .

How could she even look at me again? She couldn't. They were her *parents*.

Helena chimed in nervously, trying to distract me from

my despair. "Nefertiti is right: it's not your fault. Scientifically, a vampire becomes more like an animal when it's near death. However, even over the past hundred years, you've been able to adapt to the things Caelius has done to you. You've still remained conscious and able to resist his control. This is different. He's your . . . I'm not going to say 'father' because that, to me, is an inappropriate terminology."

She teetered back and forth on her heels, analyzing, groping to find the right words. "If you think about vampirism, or that his blood is like a *virus*, then Caelius is the original host. So him drinking you until you have one drop of his blood left is like being uninfected while reinfected by the initial virus.

"If I, or any other vampire, drained you to the last drop, you'd be injured, but for the most part conscious. You would recover quickly and be able to have some semblance of control because you are his First-Born and that strong. But this is Caelius, the 'father' of all, taking away your birthright and then returning it on his whim. It's different, Lucian. It's like a massive, multi-organ infection. I'm surprised you're not fully subservient to Caelius by now."

I could feel her cold hand patting me on the back again. When Helena was alive, her touch had been warm and firm. I knew the point she was trying to make, though. When Gracuri had fed me a small town, I hadn't been conscious then, either, but that had been because the Light was purging my blood of Caelius, the only thing keeping my decayed body alive. Now . . .

This was worse. The ownership that pulsed in the venom of Caelius's bite made me want to please him. Gracuri was the only child I'd drunk from, and it had been awful, the way it fevered his mind. How long would it take for the same thing to happen to me? How many feedings before I became Caelius's slave? What would it take, the blood of my children? Or would he force-feed me his own blood until I knelt willingly in submission?

"Kill me," I whispered under my breath.

Nefertiti and Helena were both silent in response, and Helena's patting hand froze in place.

I straightened up and looked directly at Nefari.

"Kill me."

Pain shrouded her features as she shook her head. "I would never . . ."

I shifted my gaze to Helena. "There's no reason for me to make it out of this alive. If I die, Shea never has to know that I killed her parents, and Caelius can't use that to hurt her. She won't believe him. But if I *live*, Caelius is going to use my body to harvest his full power, killing all my children in the process. He might even make me his . . . *his*! Body and soul this time! Then he'll kill Shea. Or I will."

Helena's eyes widened with the new possibilities. Nefertiti just looked away in denial of my logic.

"Helena, take Nefertiti and leave this place. Nefari—"

She continued staring at the cold stone floor.

"Nefari!" I pleaded. "Listen to me! If Caelius is using me and your father to keep you enslaved here, let me die and you can be free! Ur-Nammu is in Miami. Take him, join Shea, and stop—"

"*You* stop!" Nefertiti commanded, then stepped forward and struck me across the face. "Don't . . . don't! You can never ask me to kill you again . . . and for *her*? And it's not just you and my father, there's also—"

"I don't understand!" Helena cried, stepping between us. "I know you're against turning anyone, Lucian, but you can at least turn Shea's parents and give them back to her. You're not heartless; why wouldn't you save them?"

"What?" I reached out to grab her, momentarily forgetting about the chains. "Save them? Because they're *dead*! You have to turn someone right after you drink them! It's been three days!"

Silence

And then . . .

Helena laughed. It was dry and startling. "Oh, *that*. I've been studying our kind for some time. Of course you don't know. Here's an interesting scientific fact: a body can be dead for *ten* days before it's turned. Not eleven though. That was an unfortunate experiment."

I jerked desperately against my chains. "*Yes*! I'll turn them! Anything! What do I have to do?"

Helena leaned back and Nefertiti's mouth opened, but nothing came out. They were both shocked by the urgency of my response. But if Caelius could return at any moment, I had to save Shea's parents before he arrived. I could still find a way to kill myself after.

They were dismayed, but not immobilized. Within an instant Nefertiti and Helena had dragged in two bodies. The stench was beyond comparison. There was a word in Gutium for something that was worse than the smell of death. As Nefertiti scowled, I saw her utter it under her breath, masking the sound of her retching.

I looked at Helena. "What do I do?"

She recoiled slightly. "It's not pretty."

I looked at the purple, bloated bodies of Shea's parents. No, it wasn't pretty.

"I'll do anything," I said, trying not to vomit.

"Then pucker up."

"Pucker . . . ?"

Helena sighed, exasperated. People of intellect always hated explaining things to the lesser-minded, even if she did adore me. "It's simple: you already drained Shea's father, so you just have to give him some of your blood. For Nefertiti . . . it's going to be a bit more difficult. And it might not work. You didn't drain the mother completely; we salvaged some of her in time. Nefertiti drank what was left after your little talk the first night. Now she'll need to dip her fangs into your blood before she pours her blood into Shea's mother's mouth. It's like a claiming. A transference? No. What's the word I'm thinking of . . . ?"

"Crazy?" I stated plainly.

Helena looked at me and smiled. I didn't return her gleeful expression. This was something she must have worked out on paper, and the botanist in her was excited to see the experiment come to life. But this wasn't testing a theory. These were Shea's *parents*. It couldn't fail.

Nefertiti avoided eye contact. I leaned toward her. "Thank you for doing this, Nefari."

Her eyes stayed down. "We need you strong, Lucian. You can kill Caelius with our help. But you can't be distracted and full of self-loathing. This was another tactic by Caelius to keep you small, under his power, and hating yourself, just where he likes you. And . . ." She paused, straining. "We-we need Shea as an ally. If turning her dead mother will help that cause, I have no choice."

Helena placed Shea's father into my arms. I cringed, staring at his blue mouth. "Why is it always the lips?"

"It's interesting," Helena chirped in her isn't-science-wonderful voice. "Why can we only turn someone by the blood of our lips in an embrace? The data is fascinating. See, the tissue around that region—"

Nefertiti waved. Helena shut up.

I closed my eyes and bit my lower lip. I'd never kissed a corpse before. Not a cold one, not one that had been dead for three days, and certainly not one that belonged to Shea. Her father.

I pressed my lips against his and let my blood fall into his open mouth. Within an instant, Shea's father jerked up, gasping for air even though he didn't need it.

Nefertiti moved toward me and sank her teeth into my neck. She pulled away quickly, her mouth covered in my blood. The pleasure my body surged with when her teeth sank into my flesh was *unimaginable*. I thought I had mastered that technique, but she put my kiss to shame. I tried to shake off the sensation as Shea's father stumbled around in front of me, confused.

Then he started clawing at his skin. The first stage. Your skin feels like it's covered in ants, ants that are all biting down and chewing as the body restores itself.

Shea's father grabbed his stomach, instinctively growling. I looked at Helena. It was too soon. Usually the pangs of unbearable hunger didn't set in until the next morning, or the morning after.

Helena shrugged. "We'll have to make do, Lucian. We couldn't sneak above and procure bags of blood under the watch of Caelius. And the longer they're dead, the hungrier they are

111

when they wake. He needs to feed now, or . . ." She paused, letting me fill in the rest.

Usually, in my dark past, I'd give my children fresh humans to feast on. I'd never given my other children a second taste of their father; I hadn't been sure of the effects. But if Shea's father didn't get more blood soon, he would die again, and no vampire kiss would revive him.

I called him to my side and presented my neck. He dug in like a thirsty teenager drinking a gallon of water after football practice. I told him to stop, that he'd had enough; my blood was too rich for a new, inexperienced vampire. He kept drinking. I warned him again. I moved to catch him as his eyes rolled back in ecstasy and he collapsed, but I couldn't latch on past the chain's reach.

I looked at Helena, and she half smiled. "He'll recover," she said softly. It was uncommon for a vampire to black out from overfeeding, but my blood was infectious like Caelius's.

Nefertiti eyed me, then reluctantly dipped her teeth into the purple of Shea's mother's mouth. Nefertiti held her teeth there. Helena nodded. "Just hold it there for a few more seconds. I'll count you down. Ten, nine, eight . . ."

CHAPTER 7
SHEA

What.

Was.

Happening?

My mind was still buzzing from the liquid sunshine I'd just inhaled in Egypt. Then Meky had carried me at her lightning speed to where Lucian was held captive. But now I couldn't think straight. I couldn't see straight. The amount of power surging through every cell of my body was overpowering all of my senses. I had to be hallucinating. I had to be.

Because what I saw was my dad lying on the ground, dead, and Nefertiti eating my mother. And some strange female vampire was watching the whole thing with fascination while Lucian was chained to the wall.

No.

This couldn't be right.

I was seeing my worst nightmare, not reality. The sun power

was messing with my mind.

"Stop!" Meky yelled across the room.

She sounded shocked and upset.

That was when I knew it was real.

Nefertiti had killed my father, and now she was finishing the job by killing my mother.

Not going to happen.

I called forth as much of the sunshine-juju as I could muster and directed it all on Nefertiti. The force knocked her off my mother's body, and then I levitated her into the air.

It was too late.

My mother was already dead.

I froze for a second, keeping Nefertiti struggling a few feet off the ground. I stared at the two bodies of the people who'd given me life, who'd given me everything. Who were the kindest, most supportive parents anyone could ask for.

Molly and Jeff Harper.

They were gone.

Forever.

The pain was too much to bear.

I screamed.

I wished I hadn't gone with Meky to the sundial. Its power intensified my emotions beyond reasoning. All I could think of was to destroy the one who had killed the two people who meant the most to me in this world: Nefertiti.

I stared at her with all the hatred I felt pounding in my heart. Her screams only fed my anger. Good. She deserved to feel pain, like the pain she had caused them.

I would make her suffer worse than Caelius ever could.

I squeezed my hand tightly and watched as her blood poured out of her nose and mouth in a grotesque waterfall of flowing red.

Watching her suffer made me feel intoxicated. It lessened the anguish at seeing their lifeless bodies. I barely heard Meky screaming at me to stop, her hands clawing at my arm. The strange vampire woman with Nefertiti tried to attack me too, but they were no match for me.

Not even a First-Born could hurt me now.

With a wave of my hand, I trapped Meky and the other vampire with invisible bonds.

Nefertiti needed to die.

The once beautiful Egyptian princess was now thin flesh on bones. It was justice. She'd drained them, and I'd drained her.

Her screams stopped.

It was then that I realized Lucian had been shouting this entire time, the same thing over and over. "Nefertiti didn't kill them, Shea! I did! Caelius starved me, and in a frenzy I killed your parents! I killed them!"

It jolted me out of my power-induced frenzy. "What?"

The female vampire joined in. "Nefertiti is trying to save your mother! Your father is alive; he was turned by Lucian. It was *my* idea. I think it will work if you just let Nefertiti try. We can turn your mother!"

The words washed over me. I felt relief but no joy. My parents had been killed by Lucian, and he thought turning them would make up for it?

I stopped my attack on Nefertiti, and her body fell to the floor.

The choice was now mine.

Heal Lucian's ex and let her give my mother eternal life, or let my mother stay dead.

The searing ache in my chest decided for me.

I needed my parents, both of them. I longed for one hug, one look, one kiss on the cheek to tell me that everything was going to be okay. They may have forgotten me thanks to the angel brothers, but Aidan had said they could give them their memories back. I didn't even care. I just needed to see them alive, not corpses.

I ran over to Nefertiti's still form. She looked mummified from the amount of blood she'd lost. I placed my wrist over her mouth. "Drink."

I kept my blood free of the liquid sunshine I usually used when dealing with vampires. It didn't take much to revive Nefertiti. She drank deeply, and within seconds her face was flushed.

"I'm sorry," I said quietly.

To my surprise, she placed a hand on my cheek. "If I thought someone had killed my parents, I would have done the same."

"Can you still turn her?" My eyes filled with tears.

She simply nodded and went to my mother.

Her words haunted me.

I couldn't look at Lucian.

Not yet.

He'd killed them.

And yet, I didn't try to torture him. I didn't try to kill him. I didn't even yell at him. What did that say about me?

Slowly, I turned to face him.

His eyes were wracked with pure agony. I turned away. I

116

couldn't look at him when I felt so much pain. I wasn't ready to forgive him. I wasn't ready for anything. One thing I knew, though: the person I should be angry at was Caelius.

He probably thought it would be fun giving my parents to a starving animal, thought it would tear us apart irrevocably. Maybe he had succeeded. Could I ever really trust Lucian? What if Caelius starved him again and he started killing more innocent people?

Lucian was a vampire, and when faced with death, he'd chosen to kill human beings rather than die. Would I have done differently? I'd have liked to think so, but I wasn't sure. One thing I knew: Aidan never would. The scar on my stomach told me as much.

Aidan had been willing to kill his best friend to save billions of lives. Both Lucian's and Aidan's decisions hurt me to my core. The one who'd murdered my parents, and the one who'd tried to murder me. Both decisions had been made out of desperation, and both felt wrong, but I had forgiven Aidan . . .

At least Lucian had done the only thing he could think of to make it up to me: he'd turned my father and somehow convinced Nefertiti to turn my mother.

In a completely messed up world, it showed how much he didn't want to hurt me, that it would somehow soften the blow that he'd devoured them in the first place.

"Shea," Lucian began. "I—"

I put my hand up to stop him from talking. "I can't. Not yet." I couldn't stomach hearing explanations. I was pretty sure I'd come to the correct conclusions, and I needed to process.

Meky's voice came out of the silence. "Um, Shea? Could you

release me and Helena?"

Oops.

Helena. It was good to know the other woman vampire in the room had a name. I waved my hand, freeing them. They hurried over to Nefertiti and my mother to monitor the progress.

"Shea," Lucian began again.

I whirled on him. "I said I'm not ready—"

Dad.

He was awake now and walking toward me.

It was the worst feeling in the world. My dad stared at me with . . . hunger. Being the only human in the room—and according to every vampire ever, being the Vessel made me smell extra sweet—I looked like dinner to him. What made it even more devastating was the fact that there was zero recognition in his expression. Aidan's brothers had done their job well; my dad had no idea who I was.

Lucian's voice turned deep and commanding as he said to my father, "Shea is not food. She's your daughter." Not knowing my dad didn't have any of his memories, Lucian looked baffled as he tried to rationalize. "I'm sorry, Shea. He fed directly from me; it must be confusing him."

I could barely look at Lucian, but I had to explain. "It's not your blood. Aidan's brothers repressed my parents' memories of me." I laughed sarcastically. "To protect me." The irony was astounding as my father looked at me like I was a Big Mac.

"But she smells good." Dad sniffed the air.

Ew.

I stepped in. "Listen, Da . . . *Jeff*, you don't want to attack me. It would go badly for you." I could keep my father at bay, but I really didn't want to have to resort to that.

"How do you know my name?" he asked me suspiciously.

It stung.

A lot.

Stupid Aidan and his brothers.

Lucian answered for me, staring deep into Dad's eyes. "Shea is very important to us."

"Just don't." I stopped Lucian from continuing. Everything felt like such a mess—a horrible, sticky, hopeless mess. I couldn't imagine feeling normal again. I had thought my parents were safe. All memories of me forgotten, yes, but safe. Now they'd been killed by my boyfriend and brought back to life by him and his ex.

Ugh.

"She's waking up," Meky announced, pointing at Mom. She smiled at me as if the news that my mother was officially a vampire was supposed to bring me happiness.

Dad raced to Mom's side, touching her face lovingly.

Okay, yes, I was happy she was still alive too, but I didn't want this for her. I didn't want this for my dad. Why couldn't they be home in Phoenix complaining about how hot it was?

"What is your mother's name?" Nefertiti asked.

"Molly," I answered.

The surrealness of the situation only grew more intense as my heart seized with emotion. I couldn't do this anymore, standing by and letting events unfold. I was too angry. I was too sad. I was too . . .

Lost.

I needed Lucian, but I didn't want him. I needed to feel his arms around me and have him comfort me, but if he touched me now I'd feel nothing but revulsion. My mind couldn't keep itself together. It was still swimming with power from the sundial, and combined with everything that was happening in front of me, the power surging through me only made my confusion worse.

"Mother? Father?" My mom's voice ripped me from my thoughts. She was holding her stomach in hunger.

Lucian and Nefertiti exchanged surprised, then knowing looks, as if they could hear each other's thoughts.

Puke.

"Why is she calling you that?" I asked them with a little too much venom in my tone.

Lucian was about to explain, but Nefertiti stopped him with a glance. She was smart. I didn't want to hear from him right now. The only reason I tolerated her was because I felt horrible about how I'd reacted when all she was trying to do was fix my boyfriend's murderous mistake.

Nefertiti tried to sound as soothing as possible as she explained. "The only way to make a vampire is to drink all of the human's blood. Since I wasn't the one who drained your mother, I had to take some of Lucian's blood and mix it with mine because males cannot turn females."

"So my *mother* is now your vampire baby?" I realized in disgust.

Mom cringed at my words. "I am not your mother. I have no child. Jeff and I never had nor wanted any children," she practically spat.

Great. So by wiping their memories, Aidan's brothers had turned my parents into baby-hating pricks. Awesome.

"You may not remember because some angel a-holes erased your brain, but I'm your kid, so get over it," I snapped at my mom.

"Lucian, the girl lies. Please let me eat her." My father stared at him with wide, hopeful eyes. Gross. My dad was totally in love with my boyfriend!

"I seriously can't take much more of this," I almost shouted. With every new wrinkle in these crazy events, the sun power pulsed through my veins, wanting to release itself from my body. The more drama, the more unclear my mind became.

It was as if the sun was literally frying my brain.

I stumbled slightly.

Lucian tugged on his chains, wanting to catch me.

"Shea, are you all right?" His voice was so wracked with concern and love it physically hurt.

I was glad he was chained. I didn't think I could handle him touching me. "I'm fine. Why can't you break free, anyway?"

"Caelius created these chains out of Ashliel's bones. Only an angel can free me," Lucian answered.

"So we'll have to get Aidan here and get you out before Caelius comes back. Where is dick-face anyway?"

Caelius's small chuckle sent chills down my spine. "I'm right behind you, little sunshine."

I turned around slowly to face Lucian's father. Caelius was smiling as if watching our drama gave him immense pleasure. Next to him was a handsome man in his midthirties with short brown hair, bright blue eyes, and a slightly crooked nose that made him even more attractive. He wore a T-shirt and jeans, and I could tell he was as buff as Aidan beneath his clothing.

"Duncan!" Lucian cried out.

At hearing the terror in Lucian's voice, my mom lunged at Caelius, biting into his arm. Caelius instantly threw her off. She landed near his feet as Dad leapt to attack Caelius as well, protecting both Lucian and Mom.

Even more furious, Caelius tossed my father a lot harder. Dad hit the wall, sinking down onto the ground, unconscious.

He stared at the already healing bite marks on his forearm. "How dare you feed from *me*!" he shouted at Molly. "I choose who drinks my sacred lifeblood!"

Caelius's fury quickly turned to amusement as my mother's face went from anger to complete and total devotion from tasting his blood.

Normally, seeing my mom stare at Caelius with loving eyes would be the worst of my problems, but when Caelius turned his attention back to Duncan, I knew we were in for some serious trouble.

From the desperation in Lucian's expression, Duncan must have been one of Lucian's Second-Borns. It appeared that Caelius was finding new and horrific ways to torture Lucian. My heart broke for him. Even after what he'd done, I still loved him. I just hadn't *accepted* what he was yet. I thought I had, but having seen both my parents dead, and now vampires, I obviously hadn't. Acceptance would take time.

Time was something we didn't have at the moment.

Duncan stood stock-still next to Caelius. He seemed to be trapped under the older vampire's compulsion, unable to move or speak.

Lucian tried to lunge toward his father, but because he was

chained he couldn't move far. "Caelius, you don't need him. I'm enough! Kill me instead!" he growled. Lucian knew he couldn't defeat Caelius, he couldn't even reach him, yet he would try anyway to save his son.

Seeing my dad on the ground, knocked out cold, I was just grateful Caelius hadn't killed him on the spot. My dad was one of Lucian's Second-Borns now. Would he die for him as well?

A rush of emotion flooded through me, and I knew Lucian would protect my dad with his life. Not just because he was a Second-Born, but because he was *my* dad.

Lucian loves me.

I held on to that thought. It helped keep the surging power within me under control.

Lucian loves me.

His feral mind hadn't been able to stop him from feeding off my parents when he'd been starved, but when he'd come to his senses, he'd tried to fix the situation—for me.

Caelius loved seeing his son upset. He looked like he couldn't wait for a fight. "It took me a while to find dear old Duncan. Gracuri hid him well, but I am, after all . . . me." Caelius pinched one of Duncan's cheeks. "Hiding in plain sight on the Scottish Highlands from whence he came. Brilliant."

"You can release Duncan now," I said with way more attitude than I'd expected. After kicking Caelius's butt *before* my recent sunshine mojo, I figured this guy was toast. I might as well save one of Lucian's children in the process.

Caelius turned and smiled. "You're cute." Then he motioned wide toward the rest of the gang. "Turning the Vessel's parents. How very dramatic."

My mother stared at Caelius with big, adoring eyes.

"Mom, I mean, Molly. You hate him." I tried to give her a heads-up, but she didn't give me the time of day.

Caelius walked over to my mother and took her hand, kissing it gently. "What a lovely creature you are, Molly. The mother of a Vessel and made into one of my grandchildren by my very own Adam and Eve. Such a rare thing."

That was it.

I used the wind and threw my hand out. Caelius went flying across the room, slamming against the wall, creating a small crater with his back.

"Get away from my mother!" I roared.

Mom turned to me with a hateful gaze. "I am *not* your mother!"

Before I could think to defend myself, she was pinning me to the ground and biting my neck.

I instantly turned my blood into liquid fire, and Mom reeled back in pain.

"Devil child!" she accused.

"Me? You're the one who just tried to eat her own daughter!" I knew she didn't remember me, but I hoped there would be some kind of recognition. A flicker? Something!

"I don't have a daughter!" she shouted furiously.

Making my mother forget having a child was one thing, but *hating* the idea of having one was extreme.

Caelius brushed himself off and seemed even more pleased than before. "Just wonderful!"

My face must have said it all, and he laughed. "The beasts never seem to think things through, do they?"

In this case, I had to agree with him. "No, apparently not."

Caelius raised his eyebrow in surprise that I'd agreed with his berating, but I was so mad at Aidan's brothers, I didn't care. He looked over at Lucian. "See, my son? Even this bitch can learn."

My temper began to boil again. Using my powers on Nefertiti and then in small bursts on my mother and Caelius had only caused the sun-juice in me to surge. I needed to release the power. It felt as if I was bottling fire, and I had to pull the stopper out.

I knew that I needed to bring my parents to Aidan. He could give them their memories back, and this would all be over. Yes, they'd be vampires, but at least they'd be alive. And they'd know who I was and not be jerks.

The only thing standing in my way was Caelius.

My eyes met his.

In a panic, he grabbed the still form of Duncan, and before anyone could lift a finger, Caelius drained the Highlander.

Lucian screamed.

Caelius pounced on me.

The Light was raging inside, filling me with energy.

I concentrated all my thoughts on Caelius.

On his bones.

On the oxygen in his blood.

On the air around his body.

And I squeezed my fingers into a tight fist.

The sound of cracking filled the room as I broke every single bone in his tall frame.

Caelius's body crumpled to the floor. His skin looked like it was made of rubber with no skeleton to give him shape.

No one in the room moved.

Except Caelius, who reached his blubbery hand out for help. The vampires stared at him as if Caelius was calling out to them in their heads.

Nefertiti was the first to snap out of it. "Don't listen to him! This is our chance!"

Lucian's eyes cleared, and the intense hatred for his father showed through. He looked at me. "Shea, I can't break these chains! Can you bring his body to me? We can try to kill him!"

Helena shook out of the spell as well and yelled, "We can't! It's not time! The device isn't ready yet!"

Nefertiti looked like a fierce warrior. "We have to try, Helena. Look at him, he's begging all of us to help him! He's never done that before!"

Helena hesitated, then nodded in agreement. Meky stood at her side, ready to fight as well. That left only my mom in Caelius's thrall. I'd never been so grateful that my dad had been knocked out.

"I'm in," I said, trying to sound stronger than I felt. Crushing Caelius had depleted most of my mojo. It felt like he was stronger this time than he'd been the last time we'd fought. Drinking Duncan must have given him some extra juice. I just needed to get his body to Lucian so all four vampires could fight him. We could do this. We could finally kill this monster.

I used my power over the air and wind, lifting Caelius's body, then slamming him down onto the floor. My boyfriend had never looked happier. Lucian tore his bare feet into his father's neck, ripping flesh off with his raw strength. I was amazed at how well Lucian could fight with only his feet, his arms still chained to the wall.

126

But he was not alone in his efforts.

Nefertiti buried her hand in Caelius's chest and ripped out his heart, squeezing it until it burst.

Meky and Helena tried to tear Caelius's limbs from his body, but they weren't strong enough. Only the First-Borns, Lucian and Nefertiti, appeared to have enough power to shred his flesh.

My dad unfortunately woke up from the commotion, but instead of helping Caelius, he stood next to Lucian, acting as his bodyguard. Definitely weird, but better that than helping Caelius. I tried not to notice that my dad kept his eyes on my boyfriend like he was a unicorn. Seriously, that was grosser than the gore.

There was so much ripping flesh and blood, I felt like I was watching the X-rated version of Animal Planet.

Joining the killing frenzy, I connected to the wind again, since it was all I could manage at the moment. I sent an arm-size tornado burrowing into Caelius's skin. I could feel myself growing weaker, though. I wasn't going to stay conscious long.

Only my mother was transfixed from having tasted Caelius's blood. She watched the mayhem and torture of her vampire granddaddy in horror.

Still, as long as she stayed out of it, we could do this.

I started feeling the stirrings of hope.

I drilled the small tornado into Caelius's body over and over until he was unrecognizable.

He couldn't survive.

It would be impossible.

My mind grew fuzzy. I couldn't keep the tornado up much longer.

Faster than the blink of an eye, my mother moved.

I was caught off guard and too weakened to react in time.

She grabbed Caelius's broken form and flew into the air.

Flew!

Only Lucian and Nefertiti could fly!

My mom really was special.

That couldn't be good.

Covered in blood, all the other vampires huddled around the now-empty space where Caelius had been a moment earlier.

It was so sudden that we all paused for a second.

Then I realized that if we were going to get out of here, our first priority needed to be freeing Lucian. It was time to call Aidan.

Besides, I really needed to see my best friend.

I called for him in my head. It was taking the last of my strength. The room started to grow dark; I was collapsing from exhaustion.

Before I hit the ground, I felt Aidan's arms catch me. I looked up into his beautiful, concerned blue eyes and smiled. Seeing him filled me with a joy I couldn't contain. Even though he was an angel, Aidan was the only *normal* person in my life. He didn't feed off humans. He was pure. And I loved him. He must have seen all this in my expression because he shook his head, smiling. "Good to see you too, Shea."

I felt my strength slowly come back. I wasn't going to pass out. I nodded toward Lucian. "He said the chains are angel-lock only."

Aidan made sure I was able to stand and started to walk toward Lucian and the others.

Midway there, he stopped in his tracks. "Mailid?"

Meky stood up and self-consciously tried to wipe the blood from her hands. "Hello, Adnachiel."

"Mailid?" Lucian sounded just as shocked. "The Mailid I killed centuries ago?"

"To torture Adnachiel, yes, I remember. I play dead very well, don't you think?" she asked Lucian. Then she looked at Aidan and . . .

Holy crap! The girl was in love!

And what shocked me even more—so was he.

"I'm sorry, Adnachiel. I had to pretend to die. Caelius made it clear that if Lucian found out about any of us, he would take the punishment out on the rest of our family. My true name is Mekytaten." Then she added shyly, "Or Meky for short."

Lucian's eyes went to Nefertiti. She simply nodded. "All my daughters have been turned."

"But I followed them after the Pharaoh died to make sure they lived long and healthy lives!" He didn't want to believe her.

"You were following decoys, my love," Nefertiti explained.

I didn't like that "my love" comment, and I didn't like Meky and Aidan hooking up either. I was seriously a jealous freak right now. It didn't help matters to see my dad drooling over every word that came out of Lucian's mouth.

"Well, I'm glad we all know each other," I said a little too loudly, trying not to sound too sarcastic, then I focused on Aidan. "Can you unchain Lucian so we can get the hell out of here?"

So. Annoyed.

CHAPTER 8
LUCIAN

Aidan fiddled with the chains, but my gaze was fixed on Shea. The way she looked at me with stolen glances before finding something more worthy to rest her eyes on . . . it was killing me.

I hadn't thought turning her parents would make up for what I'd done to her. I couldn't remember their faces as my sharp incisors had torn through their flesh, only the bliss and the agony of Caelius's consumption of me afterward, only his thoughts rattling around in my brain.

I was glad. I was glad that her eyes saw me like I'd once seen Gracuri in Thebes: not as a boy, but a monster.

Gracuri. Now my eyes averted their gaze. I'd failed him like I'd failed her. He would never learn, but I needed Shea to. She needed to remember what I *really* was. It would help her if Caelius gained power over my mind. If the time came, I hoped she would be able to kill me easily enough if she needed to.

I sighed, looking once again at that rough, moss-covered

stone, now soaked in blood.

"Are you okay?" Aidan asked.

The words were there, but I didn't understand how he could *bear* to ask me. I looked up at Aidan. His brow was furrowed. He stared at Shea's dad, then back at me, shaking his head.

"I didn't . . . I didn't mean to kill him." My voice was barely a whisper. "What Caelius is doing to me now . . . I have no control over it yet. It's not safe for any of you."

Aidan's large, firm hand rested on my shoulder. "I know. You had no choice."

I winced. More than Caelius's tortures, those words crushed me. After all I'd done to him, how could he say that? I'd killed the only woman he'd loved other than Shea. Yes, she was alive now, but I had killed her, my only excuse being that I'd thought she was just a human in love with a beast. I'd been cruel. Hard. And now Aidan was by my side, unlocking my chains. He should've been burying his hands into the blood on my chest. He should've ended me himself.

The chains cracked, and I fell hard to the stone floor before catching myself. I recovered quickly, standing tall in the aftermath of my shame. I averted my eyes from everyone, their concerned gazes landing on the gruesome bones protruding from my wrists and ankles.

Nefertiti stepped toward me, but I waved, the same motion she was fond of using. In my mind I simply said to her, *Don't.*

Leaving me behind, Aidan walked over to Meky. He moved his hand through her hair, resting his thumb on her neck like he'd done in bed the night before I'd killed her. I'd stalked them for some time before ending her life.

Lamenting my mistakes was interrupted by my newest one as Shea's father rushed to my side, offering up his neck. I jerked away, knowing the display alone was enough to make Shea sick. I'd had no choice. Her father had needed to feed. Now, for a long while, he'd be obsessed with me like Gracuri had been, except this would be worse. I'd only fed from Gracuri. Jeff Harper had fed from *me*. He'd drunk my blood. I was his father now.

Even thinking that I was his *father* now was horrific. He was Shea's father, and now he was a part of me. I pushed him back as I stepped toward Duncan.

Jeff reached, grabbing the exposed bone of my wrist. He pleaded with me to take his blood, all of it if need be, to heal myself. He touched the shredded meat on my chest. I hadn't noticed while trying to kill him, but Caelius had gotten in a few devastating gouges himself, weak as he was.

I closed my eyes and focused on Jeff, speaking to him with my mind. *You will never again ask for my blood or offer yours to me. It does not matter how injured I am. Your only duty now is to obey Shea Harper. You are to stay by her side and keep her safe. This is the only thing that will bring me pleasure.*

When my eyes opened, Jeff had rushed to Shea's side. She jerked back from him, startled. But Jeff's gaze stayed captivated on mine as he nodded, half smiling, happy to do anything to please me.

I knelt down and pulled Duncan into my chest, holding him like a child against my torn-open rib cage. I rested my head against his, the blood from my chest oozing onto his mouth. He'd been my youngest, the last I'd turned. I had two other children left besides Ur-Nammu, but if Caelius had found Duncan in the matter of an hour, the other two didn't have much hope. But hope was not the point; they were still my *responsibility*.

Duncan. He'd been the part of me that was once carefree. When I'd arrived in Scotland, his had been the first face that greeted me off the boat. He'd been my storyteller. Everything to him was one epic tale that he wove together beautifully, sometimes in a drunken song. He'd been alive and fiery before I'd made him mine. And now . . . now he was nothing more than a juice packet for Caelius's thirst.

I breathed in his scent one last time. I wondered what story he'd have told if he could've described his death. It would have been different than *this*. In no version would Duncan MacCord have died so easily. In his storytelling, Duncan would have gone out to battle the Leguna of Aten or some fabled beast from Morocco while riding a white horse. Or in a snowstorm, he'd have been frozen like an iceberg waiting to sink the next Titanic. But this? No. Duncan wasn't dead. This was just another story for him. Another adventure. I'd just have to wait to hear his tale. And if Caelius continued to grow in power, I wouldn't have to wait long.

I let his body slip from my grasp as I stood and walked away. His empty carcass thudded to the floor like used meat. He'd deserved better, in life and in death. He'd deserved better than what *my* embrace had given him.

I looked back at the others. Helena had already gone to her lab and returned with supplies. I nodded, seeing terror crack the surface of Nefertiti's painted face as she stared at Duncan. My voice was low, resolute. "Your daughters will not have this same fate, Nefari. I promise. I'll help you find them. Caelius will never drink them like he has my Second-Borns. I would die first." It looked like a wave of relief moved through her as she reached for Mekytaten.

Shea's mouth was slightly open, as if she wanted to protest but still had nothing to say to me.

I addressed the group coldly, as I had done to hordes of warriors in the past, standing before blood-soaked fields of battle. "Shea, Aidan, Jeff, and Mekytaten will stay together. I'll stay with Nefertiti and Helena. We three will meet with Ur-Nammu and work together to find Nefertiti's daughters. Shea, I mean, *Aidan*, work on getting Jeff's memories back. Ur-Nammu can Dream-Walk, so we'll all use him to stay in contact and reconnect once her daughters are safe."

Nefertiti interjected. "What about *your* two remaining children, Bohe and David? We should find them as well."

I nodded slowly. "We'll find your daughters first, then my Second-Borns. Hopefully Caelius will be focused on us, not them."

Nefertiti pivoted on her heels and walked over to Shea, snatching her daughter from Aidan's side. "Mekytaten will stay with you, Shea Harper, as Lucian has said"—her voice was sharp, threatening—"but you are to protect my daughter with your life."

Shea didn't seem happy with Nefertiti's forceful tone but nodded her head in agreement.

Meky gently pried her wrist from her mother's grasp. "Mom, if anything, *I'll* help protect Shea. She can help us kill Caelius for good, and then we'll all be free."

Nefertiti was silent, but I knew that look. There was a low

rumble vibrating just under her stare. She was trusting Shea with her second-oldest daughter, but she was also trusting Meky. I'd only seen Nefertiti as a mother when she'd been human. It was strange seeing her now.

Aidan moved to stand beside Meky, his eyes still full of emotion. This was the love of one of his lives, now living and breathing, but a vampire. Who knew he'd be so fond of my kind?

I stepped toward them, and Shea looked at me for a moment. All I saw in her eyes was pain before she looked away.

Aidan's voice was loud and boisterous. "I'll get them as far from here as I can. Shea needs to rest. I'll stay with them until we can all meet again, so we can kill Caelius together and get Shea's mom back."

I met his gaze. At least one of us could be there for Shea. And she needed Aidan, his kind heart, his optimistic nature. My eyes shifted briefly to Mekytaten, wondering if she'd be a distraction and if Aidan, in his concern for Meky, would be able to give Shea the support she needed right now. Either way, Shea was safer with an angel and two Second-Borns by her side.

I thought about the dorm and how she'd punched a hole in my chest when I'd tried to take her. Only now did I wish she had succeeded and obliterated my existence. The pain in her heart was my doing.

Before I could say anything to Shea, Aidan swept her up and they all ran north. Just like that, she was gone. It didn't matter; I couldn't have said anything else to her anyway. All I could do now was offer my life in service of her Light.

Nefertiti stepped toward me. Cutting a line down her hand with a fingernail, she pressed her blood into my chest. I didn't protest as she moved her hand over my body. Nefertiti had drunk from Shea, so it was Shea's blood moving over my gashes, along the bones of my wrists. I breathed in deep, wanting to smell the crimson gushing from her hand. I'd held Shea in my arms. We'd made love. And now she couldn't even look at me. Having Shea's blood pour over me now was as close as I would come to her again.

After my wounds closed together and healed, Nefertiti wrapped her arm around Helena and leapt into the air. I followed quickly behind, letting the speed and distance from the stone chamber separate my emotions from the reality of what I'd done there, from what I was.

***

Flying next to Nefertiti distracted me from my torment. It was unlike anything I'd felt before. None of my children had been able to fly. The sky had been mine for centuries. It had been like a lonely island that I alone could reach.

I couldn't help but feel our connection as our eyes met. I had grieved her for centuries, and now she was *flying* by my side. It reminded me of our shared moments in Gutium.

My voice was low, treading lightly. "Remember when we were children, Nefari? We used to imagine we were birds and there was no cage that could hold us. Look at us now."

Her full lips curved as she smiled. It was a good memory. Vampires could dig up those old things in the brain, days that humans buried in the mess of living. We could choose a detail, and in an instant it was like walking through a vivid dream.

"One day we will fly, La-Narru," Nefertiti whispered softly, repeating what she'd said then. "And I'll be the sun, and you'll be the moon, and we'll soar through all the galaxies. Nothing will hold us down. We'll always be free."

That last sentiment changed her features. They shifted from fondness to agony. Freedom. The meaning of the word had been like a curse to her life, a lie she'd always longed for.

"The young woman I followed looked so much like the real Meky. It gave me a start when I saw her in Aidan's arms during the Viking era. But since I had followed her double, I brushed it off.

"I hadn't seen your children since before the Pharaoh died and they were released, so I didn't know what she looked like as a grown-up. I *never* would have hurt Meky if I'd known it was her. I always considered your children . . . my family. Why then, Nefari? Why did you hide your daughters from me?"

Her eyes widened as she increased her speed. "You know Caelius would have killed all of us if you'd found out. Once the Pharaoh died, we had to return to him. Our access to the world above was restricted."

Nefertiti let the memory come to life, her gaze filling with pain as she continued.

"The decoys of my children, that was all Caelius's idea, not mine. I watched as you cared for them from the shadows. You acted like a father in every sense, but they never knew your name. My real daughters watched as their decoys lived the loving lives that they could have had.

"Most of them know you and carry the fondness for you that they had as children. And I was filled with regret. I shouldn't have

137

turned them, but I couldn't lose them like I'd lost you. Now it's all I can do to keep them alive and safe from Caelius's twisted mind."

Nefertiti had not slowed down while speaking, and I matched her speed. Helena held on tightly, eyes closed, shutting out the streaks of cities passing below.

We landed in Paris next to the Eiffel Tower. Helena staggered a step or two, then sat down on a bench close by, trying to give us our privacy, visibly uncomfortable with the emotional outpouring.

I grabbed Nefari's chin and turned her face toward me. "You should have told me. I would have helped free you from Caelius. Instead I wept over every child who died. I thought it was one more piece of you that I was losing, that would be gone into the abyss forever."

She brushed the back of her hand against my cheekbone. "Oh, La-Narru, still so much a boy. I know that's what you would have done. You would have fought for what you loved most. You are just as Gutian as I am, and you would have gotten us all killed."

Nefertiti was right. It was my oversight in Egypt that had brought about my death. She was a strategist, and I was more impulsive and passionate.

She closed her eyes. Her lips moved quickly. A sudden gust of wind tossed my hair as Ur-Nammu arrived and ran to our side. My mouth fell open in surprise. Nefertiti answered my unspoken question. "Of course I can Dream-Walk; I don't know why you can't. I cryptically told my father to meet us here."

Ur-Nammu looked up toward the tip of the Eiffel Tower. "Is

Setepenre all right? Is she here?"

Nefertiti shook her head. "You can see for yourself. You know she's not."

Ur-Nammu let his hand fall heavily on Nefertiti's as he pulled her to his chest, stroking her hair as he spoke. "You knew Setepenre wouldn't be here, yet you came for her first."

I was shocked to see her eyes water, her face looking lined with age for the first time. "She's the youngest, and she's always been confused, fragile, easily misled by her emotions."

They stared at each other for a moment. "It's not because she's the youngest that you worry, my love." Ur-Nammu's voice was raw, tired. "It's because Setepenre is *his*."

Ur-Nammu's gaze turned to me. They both stared, their eyes alight with expectation. I waited, and so did they.

There was a long silence.

Then it sank in.

I grabbed Nefertiti. My hands were clenched so hard around her arms that they were bone white. I shook her hard but could say nothing, my voice trapped in my throat.

Ur-Nammu's hand reached between us. He rested it against my chest. It calmed my mind as I met his gaze. This wasn't the cold stare I'd come to know over the centuries. It also wasn't the look of compassion he'd given me in the cave when he'd pulled me from the darkness of being devoured by Caelius. This was *pity*.

I growled, and Ur-Nammu slowly withdrew his hand, understanding that it wasn't his place to come between Nefertiti and me. But he didn't move away, either. She was his world, his everything to protect.

I looked down at her chest, unable to make eye contact as I hesitantly asked, "We have a child, Nefari? A child I've never met?"

"Given the circumstances, I see no harm in you finally knowing. Yes, La-Narru, before I was turned, before you were killed . . . my youngest, Setepenre, she is yours."

I let her go and stepped back. Thousands of years. Thousands of years alone, grieving for Nefari's loss, the loss of *her* children, and they were all alive. And one of her children . . . one of her children was *mine*.

A fury rose inside me as I stumbled away from them. All of this came to me *now*, when I was hopelessly in love with Shea, my soul mate, who would never forgive me, who deserved better than a monster. Now that my heart was no longer in Egypt or Gutium, all that I had wanted centuries ago had fallen into my hands.

Her soft touch caressed my spine. Nefari had done that once before, after dressing the whip marks from my father when I'd eaten my mother's ashes. I closed my eyes. This time *she* was the one who had cut me open and left me raw.

"La-Narru, I couldn't risk you knowing. My father has helped me, with Helena, create something that can kill Caelius. We couldn't risk you destroying the plan. We couldn't risk the lives of my children." Nefertiti's voice was quiet, choked with remorse.

I turned, looking into her deep purple eyes. "I was careless in Egypt *once* when I made those sculptures of you out of mud and clay. Once, out of the hundreds of times we met in secret, and it cost me my life.

"I was a boy then. How much more careful do you think

140

I've become after my death? After yours? I've stalked and hunted angels. I've battled in and won countless mortal wars. I've changed. I've become stronger. I was strong enough to help you. You should have come to me. You should have told me about my *daughter*."

She nodded her head. "I know, Lucian, but I was afraid."

Again I was silent, and she waited. Nefertiti feared nothing, no one. She planned and survived. Looking at her face now, there were cracks in her seemingly calm expression. The centuries had changed her as well. The tortures she'd witnessed me suffer at Caelius's hands . . . I understood why she wanted to protect her children. It was better to work in secret than to have your intestines exposed at the mercy of his madness.

Still, I felt betrayed. Yes, Nefertiti had made a wise decision. But it went against the heart, and it had left me with *nothing*. All of those years with no hope of a family, of love. I'd experienced only a glimmer of it with Aidan, and his betrayal had hardened and killed what little I had left. In that sense, Nefertiti *had* left me to die. She'd left me to wander in agony through the ages.

I looked at Ur-Nammu. He'd kept his distance these past millennia as well. He'd been my only living link to the life I'd loved. "Why did you shun me?"

His mouth fell open. He'd been silent when I'd held Nefertiti in my hands back in Egypt. I'd asked for his help as we'd taken her cold body to Caelius. When Caelius had pronounced her dead, Ur-Nammu hadn't looked me in the eye and had barely spoken to me afterward.

His rejection was another symbolic death I'd suffered, another love I thought I'd killed by being the monster that I was. But she *hadn't* died then, only faked death. They had lied to me—Nefertiti more than anyone. She'd lied while resting dead in my arms as I wept. He'd known all this time, all of these ages, these thousands of years since.

His eyes swelled. "I could not lie to you, Lucian. It would only have been a matter of time before I told you about Nefertiti and your daughter, so I kept my distance." He paused. When he spoke again, his voice was deeper, pained.

"It was my fault. It was because I reached out to you in Egypt that you ended up a slave and were killed by the Pharaoh. I shouldn't have told you the truth *then*. I should have lied and told you that Nefertiti had died next to your father in battle. You could have lived a normal life, but instead you were enslaved because of your love for her. And Caelius is far more powerful than any Pharaoh. It was better that I stayed away from you. I could not look at you knowing what I knew, nor could I bear the consequences."

Nefertiti's voice was soft. "He disagreed with my decision. He always thought that you, as the father, should know about Setepenre. That it was your right."

I placed my head in my hands, covering my face. It was a childish gesture, but I couldn't look at them—and I couldn't leave. It burned in a way unlike the physical agonies inflicted by Caelius. Then I realized *this* was what Caelius wanted—not a tearful reunion with Nefertiti, but for me to feel the sting of all their silence, the centuries of deception. He wanted to sour my heart against the woman I had loved and died for.

A child, *my* child, hidden in secret. Caelius wanted to show me that all of these years he'd held in his possession all that I

142

loved. Of course, my heart turning to Shea had ruined his final triumph over me.

If it wasn't for Shea, if Caelius had freed himself with the last Vessel five hundred years ago and revealed my lost family, I would have stayed. I would have stayed by Caelius's side and served him. I would have done whatever it took to keep my family safe, just as Nefertiti had done, just as Ur-Nammu had done. Now our Gutian blood was more like a curse to me, just like freedom. The foolishness in our loyal notions of love.

I fisted my hands by my side, stiffening my back. My fangs protruded, growing large enough to rip my gums. I spoke past them. "Where is my daughter? Why isn't she here?"

Nefertiti and Ur-Nammu shared glances, but it was Ur-Nammu who had the courage to speak. "I'm sorry. Setepenre is loyal to Caelius. She was the youngest. The others knew more of you and of the Pharaoh before they were turned, before they had to stay in the caves, but Setepenre never met you. Caelius knew she was *yours*. He's always kept her close."

"Has he . . . has Caelius done anything to her?" I had to ask, but I didn't want to hear the answer. His infatuation with me was grotesque enough. The thought that he would twist that obsession and turn it on my child was terrifying.

Ur-Nammu shook his head. "Caelius is intelligent. He never made Setepenre watch your torture like the other girls. She barely knows your name, only that you are her father."

He paused, scowling. "He treated her with kindness, acting like a grandfather." Ur-Nammu's expression hardened further. We all knew that there was no kindness in Caelius's heart, only strategies and poison. "We were forbidden to speak of her proud

Gutian lineage," he spat. "She sees *Caelius* as family!" His anger boiled to the surface. "Little by little, he shortened the time Setepenre was allowed above with her sisters. Nefertiti and I were only allowed to see her once a month at that time. In the last few years we've barely seen her face."

Nefertiti stepped toward me. "It was all I could do to beg her to stay hidden in Paris."

I wanted to kill. It was night, but the city was lit up, tantalizing like a candied apple. I wanted to lay waste to it, to destroy the place where I had found myself again with Shea. The place that should have held my daughter.

"She's the youngest . . ." I whispered her name, hardly above a thought. "Setepenre?"

Nefertiti nodded slowly. "Setepenre."

My face softened. In Egyptian it meant "Chosen of Ra." Chosen by the god of the sun. Chosen by the Light. The meaning made me think of Shea. When I was with her, I felt chosen. It only twisted the knife of irony further. "Who named her? The Pharaoh, Akhenaten?"

Like mine, Nefari's voice was barely a whisper. "It wasn't the sculptures of me that you made in the slums of Egypt that led to your death. It was *my* mistake, not yours. I shouldn't have had a child with you. But I . . . I wanted to have something that was *ours*. Even as you were whipped under the pyramids.

"I named her, but I had to be clever. Still, the minute Akhenaten saw *your* teal eyes, he knew. That's why he had you killed. Setepenre looks so much like you, La-Narru." She looked down, away from my injured face.

My mistake. The mistake I'd thought had cost my life, the

144

beating I'd endured . . . it had all been because of the sculptures I'd made of her. I cursed that part of myself: the craftsman. And when Caelius had turned me, I'd shunned creation. When Nefertiti had died, I'd embraced destruction. But it was a child, *our* child, that had caused the Pharaoh's rage.

I wanted to hate Nefari, but my eyes softened. She had birthed our child: a baby girl. I imagined what it must have been like to hold her. Pain seared through my memory.

"I'm getting my daughter back," I snapped.

Nefertiti reached out and grabbed my wrist. I jerked it from her hand, growling. Her eyes narrowed. "I know you're angry. You have every right. Your family was stolen, hidden, and I let it happen. But look at you now. This urge to run off and hunt Caelius down, it's a fool's passion. Help me find my daughters. We'll join Shea, and *together* we can defeat him."

She was right. Going off alone driven by love had ended with Gracuri's head skewered before me. I couldn't let anything happen to my daughter. I deserved my anger, but now was not the time for it. What use was it to save Setepenre if she'd still be enslaved to Caelius? I had to be a better father than that, a warrior who would fight for her freedom like Onack the Great. I looked over at Helena. "We should drop her off with Shea. She'll slow us down."

Nefertiti hesitated. "No, we need to take Helena to the underground city of Amarna—the one Akhenaten built for me—so she can continue to work."

She moved her hands over my chest, feeling around. When she found what she was looking for, her eyes brightened. Her fingers curled around the gold necklace hanging from my neck.

Her hand rested there as our eyes met. Behind the inlaid stone I could feel the rough etchings of Gutian hieroglyphs carved unceremoniously by the hands of an ignorant boy. The uncut but perfect emerald-green stone that held them had reminded me of the fallen green leaves that had been by her wet hair as she'd taken me for the first time by the river in Gutium.

The first time we'd made love.

She had pinned me down, mind set on what she wanted. It had been messy, wild, and free—a taste of what I wanted to be mine forever.

The cold stone felt heavy in her hands now. Gazing at it had anchored me on so many nights to that feeling, to that hope. As time passed, however, the weight had chained me to that anchor, pulling my heart away from hers and drowning me in the depths of loss, dragging me to the bottom of an endless night that only Shea had awoken me from.

I looked deep into her eyes. "I made you this necklace when we were children, Nefari. I carved it out of emerald from the caves in Gutium. It was the first thing I crafted. And I gave it to my first love."

She sighed with the weight of the memory, masking her tone. "I gave it back to you, Lucian, the night before battle. When you left and I stood and battled for our people."

I nodded. That had been my real mistake. "You gave it back, but the first time I saw you in Egypt, as the Pharaoh's concubine, I ripped it from my neck and placed it in your hands. I swore myself to your side and never left Egypt . . . not until my death."

She laced her hand through my black hair, the hardness in her tone crumbling into careworn love. "When you thought you'd killed me, La-Narru, you gently pulled it from my neck. Like keeping a lock of my hair. It was always close to you after that. Except when you lost it, buried in Pompeii."

My teeth clenched as I hardened. She'd let me sit in lava all those years. "I eventually stole it back from a museum. But I didn't wear it. I kept it close. It was my only touchstone to my history. To you. *You* were my history. A history of silence. I almost threw it off the balcony of a chateau in Paris when I was with Shea. *She* made me keep it . . ."

I looked at the city, turning from Nefertiti's gaze. Shea and I had been making love in a villa far away from the masses of Paris, but the whole country of France had made an impression on me. I'd thought it would always be the place where I'd finally known happiness, peace.

Now it would also be the world where Nefari had told me that I had a daughter, and that my daughter was loyal to the creature Caelius. It was a nightmare, that Setepenre considered that bestial Darkness her *family*, and that I was little to nothing to her but a name.

Nefertiti reached around my neck and unlatched the chain. I grabbed her fist as she held the emerald in her hands. "It's not yours anymore," I said, the injury of her actions adding venom to my tone.

And I succeeded. The words hurt her, and she winced. But I didn't care. The necklace, along with my heart, was not so easily handed over. They were both mine now. Mine to give as I chose.

Nefertiti called to Helena, who walked over boyishly. "Great. I guess you two are finally finished talking. I would have preferred it if you'd dropped me off first." She eyed Nefertiti critically. "You know Paris is out of our way."

Nefari scowled. "I had to see if Sete was here. The others are loyal to me alone."

Helena nodded. "I understand. It's just, without this necklace we can't defeat him."

"My necklace can't kill Caelius," I said.

Now Helena lit up. "It's what we've been working on this whole time. Because Caelius turned you first, even before Nefertiti, you are the *strongest*. But I needed to imbue something of yours, something you've had in both lives, mortal and immortal. That's when Nefertiti brought up the necklace.

"I was worried about the time it was apart from you in Pompeii. I thought maybe the connection to the object would be broken, but it wasn't. Nefertiti and her daughters helped dig you out, by the way. It wasn't just *your* digging. You may have been buried for a hundred years, but alone it would have been a thousand."

"Thank you," I stated dryly. She was missing the point that I'd still been buried in ash and lava, choking and fighting death to the point of madness, all for a lie.

Nefertiti was silent as she released her fist, letting the necklace fall into my hand.

"I'm sure you're very welcome." By now Helena was so interested in her tale that she was practically laughing with delight, nudging me like the friends we'd been when she was alive, as if this was just another one of our many adventures. "I've borrowed the necklace from time to time over the past hundred years, always returning it to that glass box inside your little sanctuary.

"I'm kind of sad you destroyed that place. The artifacts alone would have been worth testing." Her eyes grew wistful at the thought of her lost research opportunities. "I kept a few of your relics. I'm sorry, Lucian, but you didn't seem to notice, and they were fascinating."

She fumbled in one of her pockets, looking for something. When she couldn't find it, she huffed, then continued, "Well, you'll see. I need to take the necklace with me. The concoction I've been putting together, a scientific wonder really, should work."

"How?" I asked. Helena had drawn me out of my immediate anger, and I was intrigued.

"How?" she repeated. "I'm glad you asked, because Nefertiti's only interested in the results."

Nefertiti gave a faint smile. "Why don't you tell him *how*, then?"

Helena spoke proudly. "Science will make the necklace harness your power *and* the power of the sun. Together it will shoot out a blast that can destroy Caelius! In theory at least."

Nefertiti's faint smile grew serious. "You're the only one who could survive this, Lucian. It will have to drain you, and the sun's power, to work. Caelius should die before it kills you. And then we'll all be free of him forever. And we can be together . . . you with Shea, me with my daughters."

My gaze softened. "Setepenre, you, Ur-Nammu, and all of your daughters will always be my family, whether or not Shea forgives me and we are together. I lost all of you thousands of years ago. I'm not losing you *or* Shea. If this plan kills me but takes down Caelius, it will be worth it to finally set you all free.

149

And Shea can go back to living a normal life . . . without me."

Nefertiti nodded, but her fangs grew despite her calm demeanor. "It *won't* kill you, Lucian. I haven't survived all of this just to sacrifice you. You're mine." She stopped herself and looked away. "You're . . . hers. I know that. But you were always mine to protect. As a child. In Egypt. And now. I am a Gutian warrior. And you, my father, and my daughters are my tribe. I will fight for what I love."

I touched her cheek, letting my hand warm her hardened features. "No, Nefari. It was I who should have protected *you*. I know that. If you can forgive my weakness, I can forgive your silence. And we can move on."

She nodded quietly. "Take Helena to Egypt then. She can show you how to get into Amarna. My father and I will find the rest of my daughters and your remaining children, Bohe and David. We'll meet you there."

Ur-Nammu stepped toward us. "I just Dream-Walked with the girls. They are all safe and exactly where we left them. Let us go find the Second-Borns together, Nefertiti."

He grabbed her hand. We stared at each other for a moment, then Ur-Nammu spoke one last time. "For what it's worth, Lucian, I know you would have been a better father than I was, but I did my best to raise all her daughters with Gutian honor. Setepenre was always more *sensitive*, like you were as a boy. I'm sorry, but I need you to be the Gutian man that you are. I need you to harden and prepare for this battle. All that I care about— the lives of my girls—is at stake. And I know you love them, as you love me. Will you fight? Will your risk your life to save them?"

150

I clenched my jaw. "I will wear the necklace, and even if it shreds me, body and soul, I will free all of you from Caelius. I ran away *once* as a boy because my father cried and begged, because *you* and Nefertiti and the whole village asked me to leave Gutium. I wasn't a warrior then, but that was no excuse. I came back and fought in Egypt for Nefertiti, for you, but it was too late. *I* should have died on the battlefield of Gutium beside my father, Onack. But know this—I will never run again."

Nefertiti's face was moved to sorrow. Before she could speak, her father wrapped his arms around her waist and they were gone.

I grabbed Helena just as quickly and leapt into the cold night air.

CHAPTER 9
SHEA

I held onto Aidan's chest as he ran with lightning speed to wherever our new hideout was going to be. Meky and Dad followed close behind. I was the only one without that superpower, so I contented myself with resting in my best friend's arms, my safe place.

Oh, Aidan, what had our simple lives become? Only months ago we'd moved into our dorm and had been going to college. My biggest dilemma had been worrying about whether or not people thought we were a couple. Part of me never wanted to leave his embrace, even though moving this fast was making me a bit queasy.

Yup. Going to puke.

"Aidan, we have to stop. I'm getting sick," I mumbled into his chest.

He heard me, like he always heard me, and stopped. Meky and Dad quickly followed suit without argument.

"This should do fine anyway." Aidan smiled, trying to comfort me.

"Where are we?" I asked, surveying our surroundings.

We were standing in open fields of grass and weeds spreading out for miles with no sign of civilization. The only man-made structure was a dilapidated farmhouse a few hundred feet away. It had holes in the roof and looked like it would fall down if I breathed on it. Seeing as it was the only place to hide within walking distance, though, it would have to suffice.

"Can we just walk normally, please?" I could hear the attitude in my voice. I was cranky, and no matter how hard I tried, I didn't want to be nice. I wanted to be angry, to kick and scream and throw a full-on two-year-old temper tantrum. Everything was just wrong.

Dad was quickly on the other side of me, acting as my escort. I knew it was because Lucian must have ordered him to. There was still no recollection or concern in his eyes in regard to me. He was protecting me because he wanted to suck up to my boyfriend.

I looked up at Aidan. "I seriously can't take this anymore. Will you give Dad his memories back now, please?"

Aidan nodded, understanding. I moved out of the way so he could do his thing. He touched Dad's forehead, and a light flared around my father's face, causing him to stumble forward slightly. It took a few minutes for him to gain his bearings, but when he finally did, his eyes met mine.

A flood of relief filled my bones. My dad was finally looking at me like a father who loved his only girl.

"Shea?" His voice cracked.

Before I could reach out to him, he moved with super speed

153

and had me wrapped in his arms. With his new vampire-driven strength, he was so powerful I gasped for breath, but I didn't care. It was the best hug I'd ever had. Probably because I needed it more than anything else on the planet.

He pulled back slightly, still holding me in his arms. "We were so worried about you," he said, his voice choked with emotion. "You were missing for months." He looked over at Aidan. "Your parents were beside themselves with worry too." Then he paused, processing, focusing back on me. "Then that man, or god, or angel—I don't know what he was—came down, and suddenly my entire life had been rewritten. The fake memories are fading now, thank God. Shea, our lives were meaningless without you. We became Republicans," he uttered in horror.

We both laughed. "Heaven forbid."

But it was just like my dad to make a joke in a serious situation. It made me feel like things might turn out okay. Sure, he was a Second-Born vampire, but ultimately, he was my pops. I felt a sudden surge of love for Lucian for turning Jeff Harper.

I had been so angry because even though my dad was alive, he wasn't my *dad*. I had still felt like he was dead. But now, having him joke with me, having him look at me like I was his whole world, his baby, his little girl . . . it filled me with such an intense joy that tears began to stream down my cheeks.

Dad brushed them away. "I'm here now, Shea. We're going to make things right and get your mother back. Okay?" He tilted my chin so our eyes met, as he always did when he needed me to really hear him.

I nodded slowly.

"Come on." He smiled. "Let's get to that *Texas Chain Saw*

Massacre barn over there."

And I truly smiled back.

Even Aidan and Meky were amused.

If we could all have one millisecond of happiness, we'd take it.

As we made our way to the abandoned barn, Dad glanced over at Aidan. "I'm assuming Nancy and Alan still have their memories wiped?"

He was referring to Aidan's birth parents. Sure, the guy was an angel, but he'd had to get to this earth somehow, and that meant parents and a family. In this life he was an only child like me, but—as I'd seen the night he stabbed me—Aidan had also had two brothers in one of his past lives: a Vessel like me, and a vampire. Gunnhild had been the vampire, one of Lucian's Second-Borns. Hard to forget a guy who'd wanted to kill me. I thought I would have liked the Vessel brother, Halfdan, better.

Aidan nodded to Dad. "My parents don't remember Shea or me."

Dad sighed heavily. "I know you thought you were doing the right thing, but Aidan, the memories may have been wiped, but the empty hole was still there. Molly and I were miserable people without the memory of Shea. So are your parents.

"When you have a child, a piece of your soul is transferred into them. Then, to suddenly live as if they never existed? We *knew* something was missing. We knew. We may not have known what, but our hearts knew. It wasn't a mercy taking away our memories—it was a tortured existence."

His words hit me hard.

And yet my father continued. "Molly was worse than I was.

155

She started drinking and leaving for days at a time. And all I can think of now is that the person *you* created is out there with Caelius. She has no anchor to bring her back to the light. You stripped Molly of her hope and love when you stole the memories of our daughter. What kind of vampire will Molly be if she has nothing to live for?"

I whirled on Aidan. "I told you taking away their memories was a bad idea," I ranted, "but did you listen?"

I stopped when I saw the pain in Aidan's expression.

He hadn't known this would happen. Aidan had thought he was making their lives better, free of the pain and agony of losing their children. He'd never realized that the people you love are more than just memories. My dad was right: a piece of your soul was always with the ones you cared about, and that had nothing to do with your brain.

"I can't give my parents their memories back. They'd search for me forever." Aidan argued desperately, as if my father's words were convincing him to undo his brother's actions.

"Then give them a child! I don't know. Steal one from an orphanage and give the three of them new memories. Anything to fill that void," Dad suggested wildly.

Aidan shook his head. "It's too dangerous."

"It's too dangerous not to! Molly was on the verge of suicide!" Dad shouted, shocking us all. "And I wasn't too far behind."

Aidan simply nodded. He was going to do it, I could tell. I was about to reach out to him and hold his hand for support, but Meky beat me to it.

Aidan looked down at her, and his eyes were filled with relief. I took my hand back before he could see it and wrapped my arm around Dad's.

I should have felt happy that Aidan loved someone who loved him back the way he deserved. I knew that someone would never be me. I loved him with all my heart, but not in the way he wanted me to.

But did it have to be Nefertiti's kid? Really? A vampire who had done who knows what over the years?

I was about to voice my concerns in a not-so-nice manner when my father tugged my arm gently. "Maybe we should give them some privacy. It looks like they have a lot to catch up on."

What? I wanted to know Meky's version of their past as much as Aidan did. Okay, probably not *as* much. But seeing those two all cozy upset me. I was being horribly selfish, but I didn't want to share my best friend. I had just been through the most harrowing experience of my life. I could barely talk or even look at Lucian because he'd *eaten* my parents! I needed Aidan now more than ever. I wanted to sit down with Aidan in that crappy, gross farmhouse and just have him hold me.

But I could see in the way he looked at Meky that he wanted to be alone with *her*.

Not me.

It twisted my insides until I had to hold back tears again.

Before Aidan could see me, I pulled my dad ahead and called back to Aidan and Meky, "You guys catch up. We'll be in the barn." I hoped Aidan hadn't heard the emotion in my voice. I'd tried to sound as casual as possible.

Yeah. That didn't work.

Aidan lightly touched my arm and pulled me around to face him.

Don't cry. Don't cry. Don't cry.

I totally cried.

I felt my father let me go as Aidan wrapped me in his arms. "Meky and I can catch up later," he said, trying to soothe me.

No.

I couldn't do this to the most selfless being on the planet.

I took a deep breath and regained as much composure as I could, pulling away. "I'm fine, Aidan. You need to be with Meky right now, and I need to be with my dad."

Aidan cupped my chin in his hand, concern written all over his face. "You've just gone through the worst nightmare of your life. I don't want you to be alone."

Right? He knew me so well. My thoughts, my pain.

"I won't be alone. I've got Pops." I hugged him tightly. "I love you, you big lug." I forced a smile. "Now go. I know you want to, and I'll be fine. Just give me the scoop later, okay?" Then I looked over at Meky. "He tells me everything, so you're going to have to deal," I announced territorially.

She actually smiled, holding her hands up in surrender. "I wouldn't expect anything else."

Her acceptance of our friendship made me want to cry again. All my emotions felt too extreme. I felt like I was having the worst period of my life. Maybe this was what pregnant women felt like. I wasn't about to say that aloud. I knew my father and Aidan would cringe with embarrassment.

I felt Aidan's lips kiss the top of my head, then we both left the embrace at the same time. He gave me a smile that told me everything was going to be okay, and I turned away before I could see the two of them hold hands again.

"Come on, Dad, let's go." My father hurried to catch up with me.

Once he knew we couldn't be overheard, he put his arm around me. "I always thought the two of you would get together someday."

"Dad," I groaned.

"Not anymore, though. Shea . . ." His tone was serious.

I turned to him, knowing he was about to say something important.

"When I drank Lucian's blood"—his eyes were tinged with what I could only describe as ecstasy—"I could feel his love for you. I didn't understand it because I didn't know who you were at the time, but I was fiercely jealous of it because the feeling was so intense. No one, and I mean *no one*, will love you more than Lucian. As a father, I couldn't want anything more for my daughter." Then he smiled his old smile. "Besides, who else can claim to be a father to their father-in-law? Huh?" Seeing what must have been a disgusted kind of horror on my face, he grinned. "Too weird?"

"Yes. Definitely."

Then his words really sunk in. *No one will love you more than Lucian.*

"Oh, Daddy. I don't know what to do."

His arms were around me before another tear could fall down my face. I was tired of crying, but my emotions were overwhelming. It was probably the sunshine juice I'd sucked up earlier, or maybe I was just turning into a sap. Both options were entirely feasible.

After another moment or two of daddy-daughter bonding,

we finished our trek to the broken-down barn. It was even worse on the inside, with muddy hay and rotted walls, kind of what my insides felt like. Dad didn't seem to notice. He found a dry corner and motioned for me to sit with him.

"Tell me everything," he said. There it was. He wanted to know what had happened to me since I'd left for college. Certain things he already knew, but I needed to fill in the gaps. I did so with great pleasure since it kept my mind off of Aidan and Meky alone . . . rekindling.

I brushed that thought from my overactive brain and sat down, spilling my guts to my father. I glossed over the romantic end of things. No one wanted to talk to their dad about losing their virginity.

Dad was a captive audience, asking me to repeat certain events. I tried to ignore the fact that they were all Lucian scenes. My dad was seriously crushing. It was disturbing, but I knew he couldn't help it. Their blood bond probably matched our own father-daughter bond. Maybe it was even stronger.

We talked for over an hour, and when I had run out of story, Aidan and Meky still weren't back. I leaned against the wall in exasperation.

"Ouch!"

I pulled away and saw a disgusting rusted nail that I'd just stabbed myself with. Great. Tetanus and lockjaw, here I come.

Before I could properly moan about my injury, my father had sunk his teeth into my neck.

I was so shocked that I couldn't respond.

My dad was eating me! Sure, my mom had tried the same thing, but she hadn't known she was my mother. Dad knew, and he was doing it anyway. He could kill me.

Well, not really. I could use my Vessel powers. But still. *He* didn't know that!

I pulled myself together and made my blood into fire.

He yanked his head back and screamed in anguish.

I would have felt bad, but my neck seriously hurt, and so did the hole in my back from that freaking nail. My feelings hurt more than anything.

My eyes met Dad's.

I'd never seen him look so destroyed.

What he had done sunk in, and he couldn't seem to process it. "Shea, I-I smelled your blood. I couldn't stop."

I sighed and then scooted slightly away from him, not wanting to tempt him anymore. Closing my eyes, I concentrated on both my wounds, and just like when I'd fixed my broken leg when Ur-Nammu had kidnapped me, I healed the injuries.

I saw my father's face visibly relax a bit, but he couldn't meet my gaze. He was too ashamed. The scent of human blood, let alone Vessel blood, was too much for him to resist.

It made me realize the self-control Lucian had. He had been emaciated when Nefertiti had taken him away from me in the desert. I could only assume that Caelius had starved him further. He probably hadn't even had coherent thoughts by then, like all the stories over the years of starved hikers who'd resorted to cannibalism. When you're that hungry, you can't think rationally.

I was Jeff Harper's *daughter*, his own flesh and blood, and he had just tried to eat me. And Dad wasn't even that hungry!

Oh, Lucian.

I wished I could tell him that I understood. I wanted him

to know that, even though I was confused and angry at what he had done, I got it. The part of me that was struggling was the part that wasn't sure if I wanted to be with a vampire. Yes, I understood, I could even forgive, but could I be *okay* with it?

I didn't know.

"Aidan, Meky!" I yelled loudly. They needed to come back. I didn't care if they were buck naked in the wheat fields getting their groove on. My dad had just drunk from me, and he needed blood stat.

Within seconds, Aidan and Meky were by my side.

I filled them in. "I cut myself, and he bit me."

Dad's shoulders drooped and he lowered his head.

Meky took a good look at him. "We have to get you sustenance. I'll go to a hospital and pick up some blood bags. I can compel the nurses. They'll never know I was there."

She reached down and waved a hand over my father's face. He fell asleep instantly. "That should dull his bloodlust until I get back." She looked at me knowingly. "And his guilt. You're going to have to help him through this transition."

I nodded, knowing she was right. And blood bags? I liked the sound of that. I really didn't want my father drinking innocent people. I knew Aidan and Lucian would never let him kill anyone, but watching my dad feed off a human wasn't something I wanted to see.

I shuddered then, thinking of how Caelius was probably encouraging my mother to kill. By the time we rescued her and restored her memories, she'd have to live with what she had done. My dad could barely look at me, and he had only taken a small amount of my blood.

I stood and brushed myself off. I tried not to examine Aidan and Meky, but the obsessive part of me couldn't help it. I checked for messed up clothing, dirt and straw in their hair, anything that would indicate a make out session. I wished I didn't feel like a jealous girlfriend, but I did. Lame.

They were both clean and pressed, like I had left them. What was I thinking? I should've wanted them to have a love-tousled reunion. I'd never see Aidan in that way, so I needed to let him be happy. He'd always be my best friend, but I had to let my possessiveness go.

"So, did you guys make out?"

I'd really just asked that. I was mortified.

Meky gave me a look that suggested I was truly insane in light of the my-dad-just-ate-me circumstance.

Aidan shook his head, smiling at my idiocy.

He nodded to Meky, thankfully neither one responding to my embarrassing question. "Go get the blood." She was gone in a flash.

Then Aidan's eyes turned on me. "Were you serious with that? You are such a dork."

With all the blood rushing to my face from humiliation, I was surprised my dad didn't wake up and try to take another bite. "Shut up," was my eloquent answer.

Aidan smiled and rolled his eyes. "No, we did not *make out*."

"Well, you should have. She's very nice and pretty, and . . . you guys seem to have a past?" I was prying, and he knew it, but come on! I didn't want to be in the dark.

"Yes, we have a past. I promise I will tell you everything, but right now I need you to Dream-Walk, Shea. Meky can't seem to reach Ur-Nammu or Nefertiti. They must be keeping a block up in case Caelius is listening in." Aidan was all business.

"If Meky can't, then how am I supposed to?" At her age, the girl had to be better at Dream-Walking than I was.

"You're a lot stronger than you give yourself credit for. Meky said that Ur-Nammu has never met anyone as talented at Dream-Walking as you are. Even more than Nefertiti." He was proud of me. I could tell.

I didn't know if he'd thrown in that last part about being better than Nefertiti because Ur-Nammu had actually said it, or to make me feel superior. Either way, I appreciated it.

"All right," I agreed. "I need to lie down and concentrate."

Aidan took off his jacket and laid it down on the ground like a blanket. Always the gentleman. "Thanks," I said as I lowered myself to the floor and closed my eyes.

I was instantly standing under the Eiffel Tower.

Ur-Nammu was there alone. I knew we weren't really at the Eiffel Tower—it was just the dreamscape he had created—but it was comforting. Paris would always be special to me because of the time I'd spent there with Lucian. Although, at this particular moment, it felt like salt in the wound.

Ur-Nammu smiled at me, impressed. "I knew you'd find me. I feel I may have met my equal in Dream-Walking."

I couldn't help it—I really liked the guy. Sure, he'd kidnapped me, broken my leg, and brought me to Caelius, but he'd done it for his family. I could get behind that.

"So what's the plan?" I asked. "Are you guys in Paris?"

"No, and we can't tell you where we are in case Caelius finds a way into our dreamscapes. But tell Meky that we're safe. We're gathering her sisters and going forward with the plan," Ur-Nammu announced, determined.

"Let me guess, you can't tell me the plan either because of Caelius," I grumbled, already knowing the answer.

Ur-Nammu placed his hand on my shoulder. It was something my dad would do, and it was comforting. Looking up into his eyes, I realized that he was growing fond of me too. It actually made me feel happy that Ur-Nammu cared whether I lived or died. "I'm sorry, Shea, but no, we can't discuss our plans, not this way. Only in person."

"And will I be seeing you soon?" I wanted it to be sooner rather than later.

"We'll see. We can't find Lucian's children; they must have changed locations. Our only hope is that they are well hidden somewhere far out of Caelius's reach." He took his hand away. "I trust everything else is going well?"

"You mean did my dad try to eat me and did Meky and Aidan hook up? Then yes, everything is peachy." I may have overdone the sarcasm in that sentence.

But it only amused Ur-Nammu. "Things will settle down after Caelius is dead, you'll see. I was wrong about you and Lucian. It appears that he has indeed chosen you over my daughter. I underestimated his love for you, and for that I apologize."

It was formal sounding, but I could tell he was trying to be familial. It was kind of cute. Unfortunately, his words cut me worse than that rusted nail. "Is Lucian okay?" My voice was small.

Ur-Nammu nodded solemnly. "He's had a lot more to deal with than his situation with you. There are factors at play. I can't discuss it here, but after all he's been through, he deserves some measure of happiness."

I was suddenly frustrated. "Then why am I here?"

He sighed deeply and tilted his head, trying to figure me out. "We must keep in steady contact with each other so that when we meet, we can end Caelius for good."

"Fine. I'll make regular checkups." It sounded a bit like I was meeting with the dentist, but that was how it felt.

If only Ur-Nammu hadn't brought up Lucian. I didn't want to think about him. I didn't want to know he was dealing with more drama. As conflicted as I was, the last thing I wanted was for him to be in pain.

"Do you want me to tell Lucian anything for you?" Ur-Nammu offered politely.

Tell him I love him. That I forgive him. That I miss him, and I never want us to be apart again.

"No. Just be safe."

I opened my eyes to see Aidan watching over me. In the corner, Meky was feeding my dad blood bags from the hospital.

"Everything okay?" Aidan inquired curiously.

"Yeah. Everything is fine," I lied.

CHAPTER 10
LUCIAN

Helena and I were in the underground city of Amarna, shrouded in robes spun of gold with strange symbols woven into them. Even with the robe and not being cursed by darkness anymore, Amarna still burned when I was inside it. Helena explained that she had created these protective robes, but Nefertiti and her children didn't need them. Akhenaten had built this place so that *only* Nefari and her daughters could survive in it. Every symbol on its walls was a barrier to my kind.

How had they tolerated hiding all of those years? And the Pharaoh had done all of this to keep her safe . . . or to keep them from me.

I'd always thought Akhenaten had hidden himself like a coward after Nefertiti's death. And, worse, he'd kept the children from my gaze. It had ripped me open, her death and the way he'd blocked me from her babies. I'd been lovelorn then, newly turned and desperate to be with any part of her.

I hadn't known that she had been *with* the Pharaoh, that Nefertiti hadn't been with Caelius at that time because I hadn't been able to enter the kingdom of light, this Amarna he'd created. All of those idols, barriers, and sun shields barring my passage . . .

I'd tried so many times to break through with the hope of ripping Akhenaten to shreds and freeing Nefertiti's daughters from his slavery. I'd burned pounds of flesh trying to find a weakness, but Akhenaten had used ancient tools of magic passed down through the Pharaohs of Egypt, knowledge he'd learned from the Book of the Dead. And, even though I'd been a new vampire, my history was of Gutium, not Egypt. I'd had no idea how to combat the Pharaoh's shields of light, nor the Egyptian engravings with their protective symbols.

By the time I'd learned—by the time I'd ransacked crypts of ancient books—he'd already been long dead, along with the *doppelgangers* I had followed, the children I had cared for, thinking they were Nefari's.

I still remembered the day Akhenaten died. The people had rebelled against him and his beliefs, abandoning the city and his worship of Aten, the sun god. I'd actually cried when I saw Nefertiti's daughters again, but I hadn't revealed myself to them. Instead, I spent the rest of their mortal lives providing for them from the shadows. And when each child had died, a part of me died with her. When they were all gone, I'd mourned for all I'd lost, drinking the sands of Egypt over and over.

My skin itched, just under the surface. It felt like thousands of beetles were crawling over my flesh. I didn't care—discomfort mattered little. I'd always wanted to see Amarna, now more than ever—now that I knew Nefertiti's children had *good* memories here, that they had been safe from Caelius in this place. I walked around, touching the inlaid precious stones coloring the walls. Everything was ornate. It was a small golden city.

I eyed Helena as she mixed powders on an altar to Aten. She was using an old contraption I hadn't seen in a hundred years. It whistled as it boiled. She smiled at my interest. "Yes, I know that in today's age you have your computers and electricity, but my heart will always be with steam. I think humanity gave up on that idea too early. Think of the pollution now—that could have been avoided if I'd had a chance to perfect some of my inventions."

I stepped closer, touching Helena's hand. "If you hadn't died."

She sighed. "I didn't die."

I flicked her ear. It was something I'd done when we had traveled together and I'd needed her attention. "Yes, Helena, you did. And then you had to spend all of your time working on a way to kill the devil, not on your inventions."

She paused at my unsubtle reminder of her living death, her hand frozen, clenching a beaker.

I placed my hand on her shoulder. "It's okay. I know how you are when there's work to be done. But you can stop for a moment. There's no one around. It's just us."

Her teeth clenched. "Not now. I need to focus."

I stepped closer. Caught in all the madness of Caelius and Nefertiti, caught by grief and loss, I hadn't taken the time to really *see* her, to process what her being by my side again meant to both of us. I set my selfish desires aside and stared. Her lips pursed, and her brow furrowed in concentration.

"I missed you." I paused. "We had so many adventures. You were the only human who ever outwitted me." I looked at her

169

distant eyes. "I'd like to think that I still know you. I said once that I would protect you, that I would fight the burdens of the world so that you could invent and create without restriction. I made promises . . ."

I brushed my hand against the side of her face.

Her whole body stiffened. "Lucian, don't."

I grabbed Helena's long braid, pulling it to the front. I took out the elastic and pushed my fingers through, letting the waves loose. "How long has it been since you've let your hair down? You only wear it like this when you're working."

She averted her eyes.

I continued. "Growing up, you always wore it back, didn't you? It was never safe to have it down around your brothers. When we met, it stayed back for a long time. But remember Tuscany? After you killed Robert and we stole that last piece of machinery you needed for your device? Remember how we rode horseback, and you finally let your hair down, the wind uncurling all of that perfection?" I laced my fingers deeper into her hair, toward the base of her neck, unknotting the braid.

Her body tensed further. Still, I knew she needed this. "You said then that you were *free*. Free from all the men in your life. Free from all the scientists who judged you unworthy because you were a woman. And your invention, the one that would make you free from death, you swore that you'd never pull your hair back again, that you'd never be something for someone else. Not for your father. Not for anyone. Not even for me.

"And I was glad, glad that I was there. To be a part of that moment with you . . . I'd seen so much of what I'd loved enslaved. Seeing you free, helping you break those chains, it was one of my

170

fondest memories in a cold, long life. And when I was in Thebes and heard that Cumbar had killed you on a train heading home and had stolen your inventions . . . I crumbled."

Her hand tightened until she broke the glass, shattering the beaker. Her fingers were frozen in its shape. I pulled a large piece of glass from her palm. I bit my thumb, drew blood, and rubbed it into the wound, healing it as Nefertiti had done for me.

Helena's eyes shot up as she spoke. "And you killed Cumbar and everyone in the city he lived in. You buried all of my inventions in the place where you thought I'd died. You made a monument in the blood-soaked spot where my coat had been found, and you went back to hating. Hating everything that was human. Not that you fully stopped hating humans when you were with me. The spark was always there when you talked about the Pharaoh and slavery, the wealthy and powerful."

I held the back of her head and pulled Helena a little closer. We were silent.

I didn't want to see her this way—walled up, hardened—like I had been for so long.

I swallowed. It had to be said. "All you wanted was your freedom. Freedom to create, invent, and travel. I never wanted this for you. All these years, you've been Caelius's slave, only allowed to work on this weapon under Nefertiti's gaze, and that wild spirit in you died."

She fell into my chest.

There was a long silence as she balled her hands into fists with the fabric at my waist. I rested my chin on top of her head, smelling her hair. It didn't smell like the fields she would ride her horse in. It didn't smell like oil from tinkering in her lab. It was

171

off, just like she was now.

"Helena. What you have on the inside, those are the things that time cannot erode, that Caelius can't touch. Don't hide from who you really are. Don't hide from me now. This work, this forced stand against the darkness, it will kill you if you let it. But I know you. Inside, you're still free, aren't you?"

Her breathing hitched as I felt a soft wetness bleed through my robe onto my collarbone.

I wrapped my arms around her, cradling her like I'd done when the scientific community had shunned her ideas as lunacy. She'd been lost in that moment, calloused. And she'd needed to cry then just as much as she needed to now—to mourn over the thought of what was going to be her life and to find the clarity that comes after acceptance of what is.

Still, crying was not easy for Helena; I knew that. She'd always been the type to keep it buried inside. It linked my heart to hers. I had learned that lesson recently—how to let go, how to escape the burial of emotions—but growing up, she'd been taught by her abusive father that crying and emotions were a sign of weakness, that love was weakness.

After dumping her off at an orphanage and then picking her up on a whim, her father had still overlooked the beautiful blossom that was his magnificent daughter and had married her off to some preeminent, cruel-tempered biologist. But Helena had read her husband's books while he was sleeping. She'd grown brilliant in his shadow.

I rested my head on hers.

I sighed, releasing my own fears at what she had now become. She really hadn't changed. It was good to have a friend, a friend

I hadn't injured firsthand, as I had Aidan. But even *knowing* me had brought that temporary freedom she had fought so valiantly for to ruin.

Our time together had been brief for a vampire, but it had been meaningful. With Helena, I'd seen moments in myself, moments of La-Narru.

She pushed back from me and looked away, gathering herself. When she was ready, she met my gaze, offering me a small smile while wiping her tears. She didn't have to say anything. The relief that covered her soft features said it for her. We understood each other in that way.

I pushed one of the buttons on Helena's contraption as it whistled, the liquid inside changing from clear to green. She swatted my hand away. "Don't touch that, you simpleton!"

She looked at me in shock as I withdrew my hand. I laughed, then so did she. It was such a natural reaction. It was as if she'd just woken up on the train and caught me tinkering with her inventions, as she had many times in the past.

Now the smile on her face matched the relief in her eyes. She was the first human to find new and unique ways to call me an imbecile. And I relished it. She was *never* afraid of me or of what I was.

"I'll always be here for you, Helena."

Her smile wavered, and she averted her fond gaze. "You said that when I was human too. You know I'll live a lot longer now, so you can't be so careless with your 'always.' "

I looped the ends of her hair through my fingers. She finally released her fists, the fabric falling lower to her hips, its pattern now more like crushed velvet than silk.

"I will *always* be here for you."

She stepped back. "How can you say such things after all you've lost? How can you promise anyone anything and still believe it with certainty? You just lost Gracuri and Duncan. You talked about them all the time when I was alive. They were among your favorites, weren't they?"

I winced at her words. I still needed to grieve my children properly. I still needed to find my remaining two. But I was stumbling, one step at a time, doing my best to keep up with each situation.

"I know I'm failing. But . . . but I still believe—"

"I know." She sighed, then placed her hand on her hip, leaning into it. "I'd like to think I still know you too. You loved them. You love all those you turn, and you love me. The problem isn't that you fail, or that you don't try—it's that you blame yourself for all of it. I've had to watch it for so long. You hide just as I do. I want you to believe me when I say this, Lucian. I will always be here for you too. You don't have to save me or take the blame. I'm going to save *you* this time."

Her smile returned. "Now go. Give me that necklace and leave me alone to work." Her smile widened. "Go walk the halls like some ghost. I know you're dying to see where they kept Setepenre. From what Nefertiti's told me, it was through there." She pointed toward a long, ruby-inlaid hallway. "But be quick. My work is almost complete. I'm going to charge your necklace with the sundial and add a few more gears."

I nodded, carefully handing her the emerald necklace. Curiosity was eating at me. The place my *child* had been taken, the place that had held my family for so long . . .

174

As I stepped inside the archway, I glanced back. For a moment Helena held the hair tie. Pulling her hair back, she paused, then let it fall. Letting her tresses remain wild as she fiddled with her concoctions, a lightness covered her face as if remembering her one, brief moment of complete freedom.

I sighed with relief, then turned away. Moving through the hallway, I saw that it intersected with a multitude of rooms. I ran through them quickly, taking it all in, lingering only momentarily in places where my family must have bathed, eaten, slept . . . dreamed.

I swept through like a tornado because Helena was right: there wasn't much time. I wanted to absorb as much information as I could. The glyphs. The tapestry. A finger painting on the wall.

I stopped.

I felt something deep inside. I knew it had to be my daughter's. I tore a chip of paint off the wall: a small blob of green. I wrapped it in a scrap of muslin. My little girl, my Setepenre.

I would keep it with me forever.

I continued to explore all of the rooms. Everything was so well-preserved: the jars of honey, the statues. In some rooms it even smelled like Nefari, especially on the bed where she must have lain countless nights while I'd mourned her death.

Everything was lavish. Had I been a mortal man, and not a vampire, I never would have been able to provide for the children like this. Yes, I would have tried, and even as a vampire I'd ensured that their doppelgangers were comfortable. But this?

I may not have been able to give them everything, but I would have *loved* them. I grabbed my chest, the pain aching. Of course, seeing this now, I realized that the Pharaoh had done just what I would have done: he had raised them here. In my absence.

I growled, darkness building inside of me. Again the word "mine" filled every thought. Akhenaten had taken all that was *mine*. If he hadn't sentenced me to death, Nefertiti never would have made her deal with Caelius, the pact that had sentenced us all to lives much worse. It was his fault. *His*. And now I was standing in the little kingdom he'd built to protect . . . to protect . . . all that he'd *loved*.

Tears rolled down my cheeks.

I folded.

I fell to my knees, clutching the small chip of Setepenre's painting. My whole life I'd been given scraps, moments to treasure. But someone more powerful always came and stole them away. Something always ripped it from my hands. And now, even as a vampire, I wasn't strong enough to protect Shea. There would always be another Caelius, another Pharaoh in my life. Perhaps that was my curse.

Helena was wrong. All of this was *my* fault. I couldn't protect them, any of them. I was weak. Worthless. She was right, however, about making promises that I couldn't keep. Why did I think the overpowering feelings in my heart would be enough to make the words true?

The weak would always be prey to the strong. No matter how I tempered my body, or my mind, I couldn't break free. My voice trembled as I spoke, a cold shiver quaking my bones. "I'll always lose the ones I love."

A soft hand wrapped around my neck as Nefari knelt beside me. Then four other young, beautiful Egyptian faces knelt around me, their hands outstretched, touching my arms, my shoulders.

Nefari spoke softly. "We are still your family, La-Narru. You haven't lost us. My daughters were raised in Amarna, but they remember the words you taught them on countless days by the river. Those times were meaningful to *all* of us. And I taught them about Gutium and our ways. Gutian blood will *always* live inside them. And ours is a proud people."

The tallest moved in closer, the oldest, the one I had spent the most time with in Egypt: Merytaten. She looked so much like Nefari. Even her voice was rich as gossamer, like her mother's. "We are many, but united we beat with one heart."

A small hand touched my shoulder and squeezed down. I turned my head slightly and recognized at once her large brown eyes: Ankhesenpaaten. With a voice as gentle as her hand, she said, "Though we fall, we will never fail because we have given ourselves over to glory."

Neferneferuaten Tasherit grabbed my little finger, like she used to by the river. I'd called her Sherit then, her sweetness revealed in her warm grin. Sherit's smile was more like her grandmother's than her mother's. Nefari's mother had come from the Zagros Mountains, and her face had reflected the beauty from that region. I could see that same beauty now in Sherit. The lineage of Nefari's mother, Shanidar.

Her words were soft. "To fight for those we *love*."

Tears welled in her eyes and fangs grew in her mouth as the last daughter, Neferneferure, spoke. "Though our bones may brittle with time, life may wear and kill the tenderness of affection, but the burning heart, the flame that is *our* people and what we stand for, cannot be stamped out of time."

There was a long pause.

They all moved in closer, embracing me, their heads resting on my back and chest like they had done as children. My family. There were two lines left. One for Mekytaten, followed by words meant to be spoken by my daughter, Setepenre.

Instead a deep, husky voice rang from behind as Ur-Nammu stepped forward, covered in a cloak. "We are etched into the very existence of all things. We are, and forever will be, a people who fight for what we love, La-Narru."

Now I understood. My people, this broken family. I understood why they'd left me suffering in the desert, why they couldn't have risked me knowing, risked Caelius killing the girls. They were *Gutian*, and they were all that was left of our people. Ur-Nammu and Nefari, along with my father, had been the leaders of that tribe. It was their duty to protect its legacy.

And it was mine.

It was my duty as the only living line of my father, Onack, and of my mother, Anna-Steen. I was Gutian, and these were *my* people. They were mine to protect. Even at the cost of my life.

Touching the girls' soft faces, I kissed each of their foreheads. I may have been weak, I may not have deserved even the scraps of love that I'd received over the centuries, but I had to try. I had to redeem myself because deep inside, even as I'd fought against Caelius's control countless times in the cave, deep within the core of my being I had always believed that Caelius was right.

Even as I'd thrown myself mercilessly into innumerable battles, I'd known that I couldn't win.

That fighting was, eventually, useless.

I'd believed that I would always lose. As I'd lost my mother, as

Gutium had lost the war. I'd lost Nefari in Egypt, her daughters, and Ur-Nammu. Then Moses and Aidan. The children I had turned I'd kept at a distance out of fear. And now I'd lost them too. One by one. Some, regrettably, terribly, by my own hand. And Shea. Anyone I cared for. I couldn't hold on to them. Like desert sand, they slipped through my fingertips.

I was weak.

At the core of myself I believed it.

So, all of these years . . . Caelius had already won.

I wasn't sure at what point it had happened, when I'd stopped believing that I deserved love, when I'd started to believe that I would always lose. But now?

Now, wrapped in these embraces, staring at all of their loving gazes, I *had* to believe again. In the Light. In myself. In *something*. I had to be Gutian again, to believe in love and its power. A power greater than any darkness. A power greater than the sum of my weaknesses. A power living and breathing in every creation. A power my father had known and Ur-Nammu had understood long before I was born.

Love wasn't our *weakness* as a people. I needed to believe that it was our strength. That we could win. That, united, we were more powerful than Caelius.

I stood up, and they rose beside me. My voice was clearer than it had been in centuries as I finished the words I had taught them by the river. "And love. Love is the soul of all that is worth fighting for."

Ur-Nammu nodded. "I'm glad you are back, La-Narru. It has been a long time since I've seen you this way."

I knew what he meant. The belief that I would always lose

had changed me. It had twisted me into something I wasn't.

Now that I was going to face Caelius again, it would have to be for everything. If I lost, I wouldn't just be devastated; it would mean that the lie had been true all this time, that I'd been born to lose what I loved. But it was a *lie*. I refused to die believing Caelius's twisted version of the truth.

I heard footsteps running down the long hall as Helena rushed toward me. She ran past the girls, but then stopped, seeing the emotional display unfolding. Nefertiti waved her forward before she retreated.

"It's finished," Helena said, holding the necklace out to me. "Are you ready, Lucian?"

I touched it, feeling its new power. "Yes. I'm ready to kill Caelius."

CHAPTER 11
SHEA

"**H**ow long are we going to stay here? It's pretty gross," I complained to no one in particular.

But it was Aidan who answered. "Until they get here."

"They" meaning the rest of the gang: Lucian, Ur-Nammu, and apparently a bunch of girls. They couldn't find Lucian's children.

Meky had just received a dream message from Ur-Nammu saying there was something wrong. He hadn't exactly elaborated. Shocker. The man liked his vagueness.

That had been two hours ago. I figured it would take them less than two seconds to get here, but I guessed they must've been trying to hide their trail from Caelius or something.

Dad was much better now that he'd filled up on blood bags. We even tried to play a game of I Spy, but since everything in this place was a muddy, rotted mess, it was sort of difficult to have any variety.

Honestly, I was mainly trying to figure out what I would do or say when I saw Lucian again. It was going to be difficult not to run over and tackle him to the ground. But I wasn't ready for that. At least I didn't think I was. The more time that passed, though, the less angry I became, and all that was left was pain.

Aidan had been a nice distraction for a little while. He'd told me a bit about his past life with Meky. It had been during the Viking days with his jerk of a brother, Gunnhild. Meky had been trying to spy on the Vessel of that time to see if his powers could be strong enough to finish Caelius off. Since Aidan had pretty much been joined at the hip to all his Vessels, Meky and Aidan had ended up falling in love. Hearing how Lucian had killed Meky (or she'd pretended to die) just to hurt Aidan only made me feel worse.

I was trying to get over what Lucian had done to my parents. Now, hearing Aidan recall old memories of him finding pleasure in torturing my best friend made things murky, to say the least. I'd told Aidan to stop telling me any more. I really didn't want to hear how evil my boyfriend was.

"Hey." Aidan sat next to me, pulling his knees to his chest.

"Hey," I answered, nudging his shoulder with mine in affection.

"I know you don't want to hear this—"

"Please don't tell me I should break up with Lucian. I kind of know that already, but it just hurts too much to even fathom not being with him—"

"I'm not going to tell you to break up with Lucian. In fact, just the opposite." He paused, probably because my face had frozen in shock.

"Everything Lucian did came from either love or hate, and the only way you can truly hate someone is to love them first. Otherwise, you'd simply feel indifference." He sighed deeply. "Lucian loved me like a brother, so when I betrayed him by killing Moses, the only other person he'd loved as a vampire, torturing me was his way of coping with the pain."

"You know, this isn't really making a great case for the guy." I knew Aidan was trying to help, but no girl wanted to hear about her boyfriend torturing the ones he used to love. "So you're saying I shouldn't break up with him or else he'll torment me for the rest of my life?"

I wasn't serious, though, and Aidan knew it, smiling and rolling his eyes. "Shea, you are so hardheaded sometimes. My point is, *I* forgave Lucian because, despite all of his cruelty, he was still my brother." Aidan's words were quiet. He loved Lucian as much as I did.

"I have to think about it," was all I could say.

"Whatever you choose, I'm behind you." He leaned down and kissed my cheek.

I peered back at Meky, not wanting another vampire attack at the moment. She stood next to my father, making sure he was doing okay, so she wasn't paying attention to us. "She's a good one."

Aidan's eyes glazed over with affection. "I know."

I felt truly happy for him. Okay, happy with just a tiny smidgen of jealousy.

I started tapping my feet. "When are they going to get here?"

As if on cue, one minute the dilapidated barn was empty, and the next it was a vampire jamboree.

183

Meky was instantly surrounded by what I could only assume were her sisters since they all looked so much alike. Talk about intimidating. They were all as stunning as their mother, Nefertiti. Lucian's ex. Ugh.

Ur-Nammu, Nefertiti, and Helena went straight to Aidan with worried expressions.

I knew Lucian was here too, but I couldn't bring myself to look. I was afraid my heart would stop beating if we made eye contact. He was a few feet away, but I could *feel* Lucian's presence as if he were standing next to me. It was the worst kind of torture. I wanted to run into his arms, to feel his mouth on mine, to see his beautiful eyes and how he looked at me.

But I kept my head down.

Helena was the spokesman for the new arrivals. "We have this necklace that we think will destroy Caelius, but it won't activate," she explained to Aidan. "It's fully charged, and it should be tied to Lucian's power as the First-Born of Caelius, but it's not moving. We thought maybe your angel powers might work as a catalyst."

Aidan nodded and took the necklace. He closed his eyes, concentrating.

Nothing.

After several minutes of trying, it was obvious angel mojo wasn't going to do the job.

"So this big bad plan of yours was turning Lucian's necklace into a weapon against Caelius? And it doesn't work?" That came out a lot harsher than I'd meant it to.

Nefertiti hissed at me. Hissed! It was more than a little terrifying.

I took a step back and put my hands up. "Don't get mad at

me. We can still take him down, can't we? I mean, please tell me you didn't put all your hopes into a necklace?" I couldn't seem to stop myself from being a bitch. It just irked me for some reason that Lucian's stupid necklace (the one *I'd* stopped him from throwing away) was their key to taking down the most powerful evil alive.

Nefertiti looked like she was about to rip my head off and suck out my bone marrow.

Lucian was suddenly between us, blocking me from the Egyptian queen. "Nefari, enough."

"Nefari? Is that a pet name?" *Stop it!* What was wrong with me? Evidently, I was possessed by a raging lunatic because I shoved Lucian away. "And I don't need you to protect me from *her*." I stalked out of the barn.

Now that I was in the middle of a field of weeds, leaving a building full of supernatural beings behind, I immediately felt better. It was like a vampire convention in there, and I was the only dish on the menu. Not that any of them would intentionally drink from me, but since self-control seemed to be an issue with their species, I just wanted to get away from *all* of them.

Besides, it was too difficult to be near Lucian, especially since I wanted him to grab me and take me somewhere far away from there, leave all this chaos behind. I wanted Paris back: carefree days of making love and just being together. Caelius was the biggest cock-block I'd ever met.

Thinking of the absurdity of that statement made me smile.

"You all right?" Aidan walked up next to me.

"You know I'm not." I decided not to pretend anymore. He knew me too well anyway. "Where's the necklace?" I noticed he

185

wasn't holding it anymore.

"Lucian has it. They're trying to make it do whatever it was they thought it would do." He wrapped his arms around me from behind and rested his chin on the top of my head. It felt so normal, like we were in my backyard at home dreaming of our futures.

"We're a pair, aren't we?" I shook my head.

Aidan turned me around in his arms so he could look at me.

I cringed. "I know that face. You're about to do something I won't like, and you're afraid I'm going to try and stop you."

He smiled. "At least I always tell you first."

"That doesn't make it any better." When he was silent for a moment, as if trying to figure out how to word his next sentence, my impatience broke. "Just spill!"

He slowly nodded his head. "Shea, I don't think Caelius *can* be killed." He motioned to the barn. "They need to have hope because they've been enslaved for thousands of years, but if it were possible to destroy Caelius, my brothers and I would have done it back when we had the chance. We were only able to trap him in that prison."

Aidan wasn't saying anything I didn't already know. This whole "kill Caelius" thing felt like a fool's errand from the start. But I had wanted it just as much as Lucian. That need to be free of his father was so overwhelming it blinded us.

I could only imagine how much worse it was for Nefertiti and her girls. They had been trapped in the prison with the monster himself, unable to live real lives, watching the world carry on without them. It must have been like being buried alive, but conscious. Planning Caelius's death had probably been the only

186

thing that gave them a reason to live.

"So what are you saying?" I asked Aidan, staying within the circumference of his arms.

"I'm saying that my brothers and I need to trap Caelius again. It's the only way to keep him from destroying everything good in this world."

"Can you even do that?" I had thought that when his brothers went back to protect the Light there was no shot at making a new prison.

Aidan nodded solemnly. "We could always re-imprison him, but we thought since he hadn't completed the ritual by killing you that he would be weak enough to destroy. Then I saw what you did to him in the desert, and Meky told me how you drank from the sundial and attacked him again . . ." He paused as if what he was about to say would offend me somehow. "And he didn't die. He should have. If Caelius had been truly weak like we thought, your powers should have destroyed him. But they didn't. Even as I'm talking to you now, he's still alive and kicking and probably killing hundreds of innocent people trying to gain his strength back."

"And making my mom do the same." I knew I should be focused on killing Caelius, but my brain kept creeping back to the horror of my *mother* being a vampire.

"Which is why I need to do this." He cupped my face in his hands. "I don't want you to tell the others. If they find a way to get rid of Caelius, great, my brothers and I are on board. But he needs to be trapped first."

I clasped his hands, keeping them on my cheeks. "Okay. But if Caelius tries to pull you into his chamber to torture you for a thousand years, I'll suck that sundial juice and get you out. You're not going to die like that."

His eyes were suddenly distant, and he was most likely remembering his lost brother. "Ashliel wasn't supposed to die," was all he said. It was cryptic for Aidan, but I didn't want to push him since the memory seemed to hurt so much.

Then he was himself again, and he kissed my forehead. "You promise you won't tell them?"

"They're going to know you're gone. What should I say?" I was a terrible liar. I'd tried to shoplift candy once. When a lady had asked me what time it was, I'd thrown the candy bar in the air and run out of the store. Yeah, real smooth.

"Tell them I went to find Caelius's location. It's simple. It's true. You technically won't be lying. You should be able to handle it even if they ask you the time." He grinned.

It only reminded me that Aidan had been with me my whole life. He knew all my stories—he was a part of most of them. No one would know me better. I hugged him as fiercely as I could, not wanting to let him go. He returned the embrace, then pulled away. "I love you, Shea."

"I love you too, Aidan. Be safe. Don't do anything heroic, okay?" I didn't want him to leave, but I knew that trapping Caelius was our best option at the moment. If he and his brothers had done it once, they could do it again.

His eyes were distant again, then he squeezed my arm one last time and shrugged. "You know me." His smile was almost sad. Before I could say anything more, Aidan was gone.

Gone.

And it hurt.

I didn't like that last look he'd given me. It made my paranoia start to grow. Anything to do with Caelius was dangerous, but Aidan and his brothers had this. They knew what they were doing, didn't they?

I groaned as I glanced over at the small light emanating from the barn full of vampires.

At least my dad was here. I'd have to ignore the adoring looks he threw at Lucian, but he was still my father, and he made me feel safe.

Kicking a stray rock here and there, I began to walk toward the shack of doom.

"Shea?" Lucian's gentle voice sent shivers through my body.

I turned. He was standing inches from me. His eyes were so unsure that it ripped my insides to shreds. I loved him so much it physically hurt to keep him at arm's length.

"Where's Aidan?" he asked.

"He went to find Caelius for you guys." Aidan was right: it was close enough to the truth that the lie had come easily. "Did you find your Second-Borns yet?"

There was a flash of pain on his face as he shook his head. "Either they're hidden well or Caelius has them. Until we stop him, there's nothing I can do." Then his eyes turned gentle as he asked, "How are you?"

His tone was so soft and concerned it wrecked me. And, like an idiot, I practically leapt into his arms. Feeling him pull me in tighter only made me want him more. We were too connected to stay apart. If that made me a moron, I didn't care. Lucian would die for me, and I for him. That had to count for something.

I stayed there with him, neither one of us speaking, just

189

holding on to each other as if breaking apart would be the death of us.

Finally, I spoke first. "Oh, Lucian, I missed you so much." I tried to rein in the tears I'd been holding back, but feeling his body pressed against mine . . . it felt so perfect, like I belonged there.

His hands ran through my hair as he looked down. It was as if he hadn't seen me for centuries and was trying to soak in every second. "I thought you'd never"—his voice cracked with emotion—"I thought you'd given up on me."

"I tried." I wiped away my tears. Seeing him there, with his bright turquoise eyes looking at me with such love and hope, it filled me with so much happiness. For once, in a very long time, I felt like things might just turn out okay. "I love you too much, you stupid jerk."

He smiled, relief flooding over every one of his beautiful features. "I love you more than my own life."

"You have pretty low self-esteem, so that's not really a compliment," I joked.

Lucian laughed. A real, honest laugh. I hadn't heard him do that since Paris.

Then he kissed me.

A kiss that made my whole body go numb with the sensation. It was blinding and freeing all rolled into one. No one could make me feel the way Lucian did. Everything melted away into that kiss. Nothing had any meaning except the two of us embracing in the darkness.

Then suddenly it wasn't dark anymore.

Like a giant beacon of light, Lucian's necklace glowed. It

brought the whole gang outside of the barn.

Our lips parted as we realized what had happened.

Helena broke the silence. "The necklace works!" Then she hit her hand on her head as if figuring it all out. "Of course. It takes the First-Born male and the first female Vessel." She was grinning from ear to ear. "This is it. We can finally kill Caelius!"

Everyone was beyond thrilled at the revelation, except Nefertiti. She could barely look at us. She had seen us kiss, and it must have cut her deep. I felt horrible. I knew that Lucian and I belonged together, but they had too, at one time. They loved each other. I'd always be envious of their history, but seeing the way Lucian looked at me, I knew there was no choice for him. I was it. And Nefertiti saw it too.

"Aidan went to find where Caelius is hiding. He'll Dream-Walk with Shea when he finds him," Lucian informed the others.

"Great. Let's make sure we can activate this baby on the spot when we take him down." Helena was beaming with excitement.

"Um," I muttered. I didn't think I should keep Aidan's secret anymore, especially if this necklace would actually work. What if he and his brothers actually got hurt trying to imprison Caelius again? If we could kill him, then Aidan's brothers wouldn't have to leave the Light. They could keep guarding it and let us do our thing.

Lucian's hand intertwined with mine for support. "What is it, my love?"

The way he said "my love" made me want to pass out right there. Damn him and his ridiculously sexy voice.

I broke the news. "I wasn't supposed to say anything, but now that this thing actually works, Aidan didn't only go to track

Caelius for us. He went to go trap him again." Before anyone could get mad, I continued. "He thought it would be better if Caelius was in one place, to make it easier for when we found a way to kill him."

Lucian's face went still.

I felt a lump forming in my throat.

Something was wrong.

Very wrong.

"I knew he was going to do something stupid!" Meky yelled. "He kissed me like he was saying goodbye forever, but I talked myself out of worrying!"

The sinking sensation only grew in the pit of my stomach. I had thought the same thing when Aidan left, but I'd rationalized it away as well.

"What aren't you telling me?" I choked out.

Lucian's hands slightly shook as he explained, "Shea, Aidan had six brothers before Caelius, not five. That sixth brother, Herostel, was earthbound, like Aidan is now: an angel in human form to watch over the humans. In order to trap Caelius, the earthbound brother had to sacrifice himself to *create* the prison. The prison itself is made from his *soul*."

Oh, God.

No.

Lucian only confirmed my worst nightmare when he finished, "Aidan is now the earthbound angel. Shea, he would have to give up his *soul* to imprison Caelius. It would be worse than death. He'd be stamped out of existence."

Everything went black as I lost consciousness.

CHAPTER 12
LUCIAN

"Shea . . Shea . . ." I ran my hands through her pale blond hair. "You're okay. I've got you."

"Aidan," she mumbled in her sleep.

I winced. Shea's first thought, her first concern, was for *him*. That idiot. Of course he'd tell her and not the rest of us. He knew the kind of monster I was. I'd never let him sacrifice his life, even if it meant saving the world. Hot and cold, it was how I ran. Even when I'd hated him, I hadn't let anyone touch him. Aidan had been *mine* to kill then. But I never had. I'd watched him choose that fate himself, over and over, killing the Vessels.

It was infuriating, his loyalty to the greater good. Thinking back on it now, I realized that I'd been waiting: waiting for Aidan to finally understand why I would never have killed Moses, why I *couldn't* have killed him, that some people were worth letting the world burn for.

When Aidan had stabbed Shea, I'd caught a glimpse of it:

his regret. Then when we'd battled over the ocean, when he'd apologized, I'd seen it again. After we'd knelt side by side and begged for Shea's life at the feet of Caelius, I knew he finally understood.

And now look what he'd done with that knowledge. I knew it wasn't for "the good of mankind." When the necklace hadn't worked, when things had looked bleak, he must have decided then. This time Aidan, that stupid beast, was going to sacrifice himself, not for the world, but for *us*: the fools he'd grown to love.

Shea shot up, shoving me back. "Where are we? This is our room in Paris, Lucian. What the hell? We don't have time for this! We have to save Aidan!"

"It's not Paris—" Again she pushed me back as I tried to comfort her. "Shea, listen to me. We're Dream-Walking."

She paused for a moment, then took a deep breath. "We are?" She looked around. "Oh, yeah, I guess we are."

I half smiled. "I'm not as good as you are. I'm sure if it was *your* dream it would be seamless. You've pulled me into your Dream-Walks but I've never actually Dream-Walked myself; that's not a power I have. I'm not even sure this counts. I think I just pulled you into a fuzzy memory."

Shea looked around at some of the blurred objects. The only pieces in focus were the bed and the view from the window, the things I remembered most. Other than her. Every feature on her face was crystal clear and beautiful.

"Why are you doing this?" she asked, looking puzzled, uncertain of my intentions.

"You passed out. No one could get through the thick wall of

darkness in your mind, not even Ur-Nammu. It's like a fail-safe, an empty barrier that protects the Light inside of you while your body is . . . comatose."

She nodded slowly, understanding, then asked, "How did *you* get through?"

I stepped closer, breathing her in. Her scent was soft and warm, like this dream. "Because I've been in this kind of empty place before, this vacuum. It will always be a part of me.

"When I was dissolving into Caelius in the cave, before Ur-Nammu saved me, everything was fragmented like this space inside your mind, tearing apart all reason and form. The scraps that I held on to the tightest were my moments with you. If Caelius had taken those pieces, what was left of my hope, I would have been lost forever in *his* void.

"And now I can only imagine what your mother must feel, having given birth to and raised the Light, and now you are simply . . . gone."

Shea crumbled into my arms, crying out. "We have to save them! We'll get Aidan and then he can give my mom back her memories!"

"Of course." My heart ached for her. I felt so helpless. It was taking all of my strength to fight the blackness seeping in and destroying this memory. I knew that if she didn't wake up soon, if we didn't get out, I'd die here and Shea would sleep forever.

She looked up at me, sniffling. "Well? Let's go."

I shook my head. "Shea, I never wanted to touch that emptiness again. But when the others couldn't get through to you, I threw myself inside your mind. Where we are now, this is *your* void. *I* can't get us out."

195

Panic crossed her features. I stroked her hair, uncertain if I should tell her the full truth. "When I first entered, I started dissolving, like I had with Caelius. I reached for this memory in the darkness, and I appeared here when you did. But you were asleep. I've been waiting. Time isn't real in this place, but it feels like I've waited for hundreds of years, just holding you while you slept, keeping the darkness from swallowing us whole."

Shea's mouth fell open. "What? Seriously? That's awful." Guilt rushed over her features. "I meant the time thing, not the holding me part."

I shrugged lightly. "I had a beautiful view."

Her eyes quickly turned away from me, to the window, but mine stayed on her. It had healed me in a way, all of that time sitting in silence with Shea in my arms. But we had to leave. I'd been trying to wake her for some time. My strength was waning, and I needed to save Aidan as well. I owed him that much. I loved him that much.

And Nefertiti, her children. And Setepenre. As happy as I could be just holding Shea for eternity, we had friends and families worth fighting for. Worth dying for.

Shea was rallying quickly. "Well, now that I'm awake, I mean, strong enough to Dream-Walk with you, let's get back."

She closed her eyes.

Nothing happened.

She squeezed her hands into fists, clamming up. "Why isn't this working?"

I shrugged. "I've been focusing all my energy on this place to keep it from dissolving. You're still weak from when you used the sundial. Its power came with a high price." I rested my hand on her cheek, a sharp pain twisting in my chest. "I think it almost killed you, Shea. When's the last time you really slept?"

"I don't remember. I mean, time is all jumbled up, it's . . . been a while."

"Your body is exhausted. I was worried—you had no heartbeat. That's why I leapt inside to follow your consciousness as deep as I could, to find you and bring you back."

Shea closed her eyes and felt her chest for a moment. Then, opening her eyes again, she shook her head. "Don't worry, Lucian. I'm very much alive. I can feel my juices rattling around. I just need to wake up so we can get back into the real world."

She began walking around the vague, dreamlike room. Every place she stepped filled in with detail, became crisp, clear. Shea smiled. "I think I have a better memory of this place than you do."

She touched a table, and the swirls of wood filled in. The lamp she brushed by turned canary yellow. Shea's power was filling in the void. It was strange, though, because the clearer everything was, the less real it started to feel.

When everything was just like the night I had left to save Gracuri, she stopped. "This is what it all looked like, but we're not leaving the dream. This is how it's done, you gain control, I . . ." She looked at me with confusion. "I don't understand, this should have worked. Why am I not waking up?"

I touched the small of her back, half smiling. "There's one more memory to fill in."

Her cheeks flushed. "We don't have time for that. Even if there is no 'time' here."

I nodded. "I know." And her fear wasn't because of Aidan or

Caelius. Shea was afraid of *us*, was terrified of reconnecting with me and having her heart ripped open again.

I understood her trepidation. I still couldn't face what I'd done to her parents. And I still couldn't fully believe that we would win, that I could stand against Caelius and actually succeed. I needed to believe that it wasn't my fate to lose her. But I was afraid.

Afraid that if I failed, Caelius would use me to destroy Shea. Poised against that possibility, I knew it would be better if she stayed away from me, better, even, if she hated me.

Her lips landed softly on mine.

I wrapped my arms around her.

How could she still love me? How could Aidan? By now they'd both seen the monster inside.

"Lucian," she whispered. "I *need* you."

My mind stopped. Nothing else mattered. I pinned her to the floor. Her back arched under the weight of my hips. I let my lips seep into the small of her neck. I *needed* her. More than she knew. "Shea Harper, you saved my soul from darkness."

That was enough. She moaned, and my spine stiffened. I felt every muscle in my body come back to life as she ran her hands over them. She bit my bottom lip as she tore off my shirt. I raked my hands over the small blue dress she was wearing, tearing it open at the sides.

Her hips lifted to mine as her mouth moved to my ear, her hands slipping off my buckle. I eased into her. Gently at first, but then the torrent of our passion broke the wooden floorboards under her back.

Shea rolled me over, and we laughed at the absurdity of

anything breaking in a dream. Still, by the time we were finished, the room looked like it had been hit by a tornado.

She lay against me, naked, panting for breath. Her eyes met mine as her soft face filled my view. She was everything I had always wanted: a love that was more powerful than death.

"I think I needed that," she said with a laugh.

I nodded. With all the madness, it was a moment of bliss. A reconnection.

"Shea, I love—"

We were back, out of the dream. I was blinking, holding her body outside of the barn, surrounded by my Gutian horde and Helena.

Jeff Harper reached for us. "Are you all right?"

Shea and I exchanged looks. I wasn't sure if Jeff was asking me or her, but I bit my tongue. Yes, we were back. Back to what our lives had become after Paris.

Shea sighed. "I'm fine, Dad. And *Lucian's* okay too."

I grinned. I was more than okay. We shared another look, and her smile matched mine.

Nefertiti stepped toward us and placed a hand on my shoulder. "How did you get through the barrier? How did you get her to wake up?"

I paused for a moment, unable to answer.

Shea stood up, her face flushing.

Nefertiti backed off. She probably figured out the "how" in an instant after seeing our shared glances and masked her concern with apathy.

Shea fumbled her words. "How long was I out?"

Meky stepped forward, her face wracked with worry. "You've

been unconscious for two hours. You were out for an hour before Lucian went in. Once your heart slowed, then stopped, we weren't sure what was happening."

We'd been making love for a while in the void, enough time for Shea to recharge mentally. Luckily, it had only been a few short hours.

Shea nodded. "We have to get to Aidan." She looked at me, and I nodded in agreement. If I knew Aidan, he'd already talked to his brothers by now and had convinced them of what needed to be done—at the cost of his life.

Shea started to walk but stumbled slightly. "I need to juice up," she said quickly. "Meky, can you take me?" Her voice was resolute.

I spun on my heels, grabbing her arms. "Are you out of your mind, Shea?" Despite myself, I was shaking her, my fangs growing. "This little blackout was the aftermath of the sundial! I'm not going to let you risk your life like that again! You woke up this time, but—"

Nefertiti stepped in. "She's right, Lucian. If it takes the two of you to power the necklace, the more power she has, the better chance of it working."

Helena chimed in. "It's the *only* way the necklace will work."

"Thank you for your *scientific* analysis," I growled, "but no, we're not saving Aidan at the cost of Shea." It was *my* life that I was willing to risk, not hers.

Shea stroked my back like she'd done moments ago in our dream room in Paris. "This is Aidan we're talking about, Lucian. Nothing you can say will change my mind."

I stopped. This was wrong. I turned back to Helena. "What's

the theory? We distract Caelius, then Shea shoots her power into the necklace while I'm wearing it, then the necklace uses that power and leaches all of my own to kill Caelius? And it won't hurt Shea?"

Helena began to answer, but Shea interrupted. "Wait. What do you mean leaches all of your power? Are you saying the necklace could kill you?"

Helena shook her head. "No. Because Lucian is the First-Born of Caelius, it shouldn't *kill* him, technically speaking. And it shouldn't kill you, either, Shea. There. Two questions answered. Now can we please start planning our attack? I have other experiments and a life to get back to once this is all over."

Shea listened to Helena, and in her eyes I could see the resolution. Then she stepped toward Meky. "Let's go. Carry me."

I moved between them. "You're coming with me, Shea, not with Mekytaten."

Shea's mouth fell open, ready to protest, but nothing came out. I turned to the others.

"Get ready for battle." I paused, looking at Nefertiti's children, then at Helena and Jeff. "Nefari . . . your father, you, me: we're Gutian leaders. This is in our blood. But everyone else should stay here. They need to be safe. We can't risk their lives. I *won't* risk their lives."

Nefertiti nodded, agreeing. Warmth returned to her features, and relief.

"We are Gutian too!" Meky said, ready to protest, her sisters grumbling in support.

Nefertiti waved. They were all silent as she said, "My children, you are the last of the Gutians. We need you to carry on our legacy. No matter what happens. If we succeed, you are finally free, a gift I've always wanted to give you. If we fail, Caelius will think that you are all still loyal to him. And you can survive. You can plan."

They nodded in reluctant obedience, but I could feel Nefari's rebellious warrior blood pumping in their veins. Every one of them wanted to fight.

Helena leaned into her left hip, resolute in her defiance. "Sorry, Lucian, but this is one adventure I wouldn't miss for the world. And I'm keeping my promise. My invention *will* save you." Her jaw hardened, but in her eyes there was a softness. "I haven't forgotten, you know, the way you stood by my side when I presented my inventions to the scientific council. I was human and afraid—they might as well have been Caelius in my ignorance then. But you stood in full daylight, steaming in the gray shadow of a pillar, just to be there.

"This time, when you're by my side, I won't fail. My invention will work. I'll make sure that it does." Her eyes weren't on Nefertiti, but locked on mine.

I smiled. "I don't doubt your intentions or your invention, Helena, but I need you to—"

"Don't."

"I *need* you to stay behind."

"Need? You *need* me there. I invented the damn thing powering that necklace!"

"And you don't know for certain if it will kill Caelius."

Helena had no answer; the scientist in her believed in the theory of her invention but knew it was only a theory. Untested. I could see the hurt in her eyes at the implication.

Her face sagged, so I softened the blow with my next words. "If we fail, I need you safe. You're the only one I trust to work with the girls."

It was too much to ask, and I knew it. If we died, I was asking her to dedicate her existence into looking after Nefertiti's children.

She looked down, refusing eye contact.

I left Shea's side and flicked Helena's ear. She looked at me with fury, that wild spark igniting in her. "Lucian, I will make it work if I'm there!"

"No, Helena. Shea and I will power the necklace—that part of your invention has already been proven. We don't need you there."

"Lucian, I can—"

"Not just for their sake, Helena, but for yours. I believe in you. I always have, even in Lorreto. If this necklace doesn't work, your brilliant mind will. Eventually you'll find a way to kill him and free yourself."

Her fists balled at her sides. She gritted her teeth, her anger willfully kept under the surface. "Lorreto? I don't know what you're talking about. This argument is cyclical and taking up time." She didn't call me an idiot, but her furrowed brow and the sneer of her lips did it for her. "If you don't want me there, that's fine. I'll start working on another way, just in case the necklace fails."

That last word hung in the air, and I could see it deflate the belief previously burning in her gaze. "I'll start working now. Just in case." She pulled a piece of elastic out of her pocket and tied her hair back. "Good luck." She turned and left us without a second glance.

Now I felt her pain. I needed to believe that our plan would work. And I did. I just didn't believe that, if we all went, everyone would live. But seeing Helena so defeated, as if it might fail, seeing her pull back her wild tresses in slavery . . . I was again filled with doubt.

Jeff spoke up, his voice small, his eyes pleading. "If my wife is there, I have to be too. Don't make me stay behind, Lucian. Please."

But it was Shea who answered him. "Dad, Caelius will use your love for Mom against you. You're too young as a vampire; he could give you some of his blood and make you his mind puppet in a heartbeat. He could make you kill her, or me, or *Lucian*." Shea apparently threw that last part in because she still wasn't sure if his vampire bond was more powerful than his fatherly one.

Jeff was on the verge of arguing, but then nodded slowly. Shea reached out and hugged him. "We'll be back for you, Dad. I promise."

"I can't lose you again. I just got you back." Jeff's face was pained.

"I can't lose you either," Shea said with determination.

It was enough for Jeff. He kissed the top of her head. "Come back to me."

My shoulders sagged, doubt of our success still plaguing my mind as Shea reached for my hand. "Let's go then," she said.

I nodded.

Ur-Nammu looked at Shea. "Nefertiti and I will search for Aidan. We'll send you his location as soon as we find him. When we've regrouped, we'll kill Caelius."

That was all I needed. I held Shea in my arms and flew into the air. I'd never flown so fast before. I kept her head carefully pressed to my chest, my hand covering her eyes so that she wouldn't get the urge to look. If she did, she might get sick.

We landed in Amarna, and I walked to the pillar and traced my fingers over the symbol of Aten just as Nefertiti had told me. It glowed bright, and the door opened.

I threw on the cloak Helena had made and led Shea underground. I brought her to stand at the apex of the Pharaoh's secret chamber. We stood in front of the sundial where a single thin shaft of light from a precise hole drilled painstakingly through layers of rock illuminated it. I gritted my teeth, imagining the poor slaves the Pharaoh had forced that job upon.

"Let's do this," she said, gripping my hand tighter and walking toward the bright circle.

Before she could touch the sundial and activate its power, I grabbed her. "I'm still not sure of this, Shea. I always lose. I can't keep the people I love. The fact that you can look at me, that you still love me, is beyond my comprehension. But I *want* to believe . . . I *need* to believe—"

She kissed me. I closed my eyes. I *couldn't* lose her. I had to stop this.

Instantly my lips started burning. I jerked back, releasing Shea. She'd set her hand on the sundial mid-kiss. She must have known that I was changing my mind, that I wasn't going to let her do it.

I tried to grab her, but my fingers blistered.

Her eyes widened as light shot into them. The light moved into her mouth, into every pore. Ignoring the pain of touching her, I tried to pull her back, but the power pushed me aside, burning my skin. It filled me with fury. The same Light-born fire had defeated me when the Pharaoh had moved Nefertiti's children down here and I'd tried to follow.

"Lucian!" she screamed. Something was going terribly wrong. The Light was out of control. "It's too much! I can't stop!"

I lunged in. Now I screamed.

It was worse than when I'd filleted myself with the Enochian blade to track her. The light burned me from the inside.

Still, I didn't stop.

I could smell the meat, the singed flesh as my skin charred.

I held on.

"Lucian!" she cried out.

"Shea! I have you!" I answered through fire-seared lips.

I pulled through the maddening pain. I was burning alive, dying. I saw her desperate eyes, Shea's desperate belief in *me*.

I *pulled*.

As she came away from the sundial, we both collapsed on the floor.

I couldn't hold her any longer. I couldn't move. I was a black piece of coal.

But now I had hope. If being in that pure blast for one moment had injured me this much, I hoped the necklace might be enough, combined with the sundial's power, to kill Caelius. I couldn't die. Not yet.

Shea jerked up, recovering, taking in a deep breath. Then, seeing my charred remains, she screamed, "Lucian!"

She grabbed my arms, but the muscles fell off in chunks. She screamed again.

I couldn't speak. My vocal chords were fried. I was in agony but no longer without hope. And I knew now that as long as one drop of Caelius's blood remained, I would recover. I wanted to tell her that I could heal, that it was possible.

Shea placed her neck to my blackened lips. "Take what you need!"

My fangs instinctively grew, but I retracted them quickly. This wasn't the same as with Caelius. Even half-alive, as I was now, I could control myself. With Caelius it had been different—his draining had been like a fevered infection that pushed me to devour mindlessly. But I wasn't his chained puppet now. And I would *never* drink Shea.

"Lucian!" Shea shouted. "You have to! I let Nefertiti drink me for God's sake! Just do it!"

She pushed her neck closer, but I refused. I had never taken blood from Shea. I couldn't lose that. It was one of the scraps I had clung to in the darkness. I'd never been a vampire with her, just a man: the real me, alongside the monster.

She closed her eyes, frustrated. When she opened them again, they were focused. Shea began to move her hands over my body, obviously having to fight back the repulsion as strips of my flesh peeled off. "If I can heal myself, I can heal you," she said, as much to convince herself as to reassure me.

Her certainty grew stronger as all of that radiant Light inside of her bounced around like pulses of power, filling the room with brightness. Had I not known her, had I been just another vampire, it would have been terrifying.

Then it burned. As her hands moved over my skin, it burned worse than Pompeii. I screamed in agony. Tears dripped from

Shea's cheeks as she continued. I was finally able to move my neck, and I watched as new flesh formed, as the marrow in my bones filled in.

I could heal quickly, but wounds like this would usually take months, or oceans of blood. Now, being healed by Shea's power, within moments I was fully restored. She smiled triumphantly.

I pulled her into my arms. "Shea, are you all right?"

She was silent. Then she pushed me back. "Am *I* all right, asks Mr. Charbroiled?"

I smiled. "You said it was too much, that you couldn't stop."

She jabbed my side. "Maybe you were right about the sundial. It's dangerous. But we need to get Aidan and my mom. And we need to kill that a-hole Caelius."

She looked at me, but her eyes were again filled with horror. "Lucian!"

I couldn't respond. Her features faded away.

Everything was black.

Then I was by a small river in Gutium, next to the house where I'd grown up.

I reached down, letting the river's water move through my fingertips. It wasn't wet or cold. This was a dream. A *forced* Dream-Walk. This river had dried up and died, like I had, ages ago.

But no one was here. I looked around. "Shea?"

Silence.

Someone had pulled me into this dream, someone powerful.

I walked around the riverbanks, not daring to go inside the small house. I didn't want to see it. It was a memory I didn't like to think of: the house where my mother had died.

"Lucian!" someone called, but it was distant.

I ran toward the voice.

I ran *slowly*.

Whoever's dream I'd been pulled into, my vampire powers were useless; I was mortal.

I ran harder, but my legs ached. My *small* legs.

I looked at my hands, at my little fingers. I was a boy. This was a very old memory. "Nefari!" I shouted. "Where are you?"

Something was wrong. These were her memories. She should have been right by my side when she summoned the dream.

"La-Narru!" She wasn't calling me.

She was screaming.

I ran. There were splotches of emptiness, spots of memory that weren't filled in. They were vacant or out of place. Memories were mixed, shifting, out of control.

Now I was grown, the age I had been when I'd left my homeland.

I must have crossed our entire forest before I came upon the empty field by Gutium. And there they were, all of my people, the Gutian tribes . . . slaughtered.

This memory was vivid. Every detail. The smell of death. The ache of defeat. I took in the massacre. I'd never seen it; I hadn't been there. I'd wept for the loss of my people but had never returned to Gutium. It had been isolating, bearing the weight that I was the only Gutian left in the world. I'd been a young man, but it had been devastatingly lonely. The hum of the code of my people, decaying my heart with guilt. When I'd found Nefertiti and her father *alive* in Egypt I'd been overtaken with relief and vengeance.

Now, seeing this, I finally faced my shame. I should have been here, with my people, with my father, Onack. On the field of slaughter I recognized the rich blue fabric of his cape. His frame, a large mound surrounded by hundreds of dead Egyptians. Nefertiti had *seen* all of this. Lived it.

I walked over to him: Onack the Great. Twenty spears had been shoved through his body like a stuck pig. His sword was still clenched in his fist, even after death. I fell to my knees by his side, tears forcing their way down my cheeks.

"I'm sorry, Father." I rested my head on his chest. I should have been here. I should have fought and died by his side.

After he'd whipped me for eating my mother's ashes, I'd never forgiven him—because I'd never forgiven myself. When he'd begged me to leave, I'd hated him for it. These were childish things I'd unknowingly held on to all of these years. But seeing him now, dead . . .

He'd died *alone,* without his family by his side.

My father. My *real* father.

"La-Narru!"

I jerked up. Nefertiti was on the battlefield, covered in blood. I rushed to her side. "Why are you dreaming this? What's happening?"

Her voice was soft, weak. "We found Aidan. He was trying to summon his brothers. We were telling him about the necklace, how it works now, when Caelius showed up and ambushed us.

"We're mid-battle. I pulled you in here because this is my most powerful memory, and this is where we are. You may not recognize it now, but it's the field by our village where you used to pick wildflowers for me in the spring. It's all I can do to get this message to you before—"

I was staring at Shea. The dream had disappeared as quickly as it had come. She was shaking me, repeatedly calling my name.

"I'm here, Shea. I'm here."

"What the hell happened, Lucian? Your eyes went black and then you were just gone!"

"Caelius has them: Aidan, Nefertiti, and Ur-Nammu. We need to go, *now*." I pulled her into my arms.

Shea nodded. "Okay. I'm ready."

I flew toward my home. I didn't doubt that this place had been handpicked by Caelius. The battle I never got to fight was here, now. Except this time I wouldn't run.

When I landed in what used to be Gutium, the scene was similar to the massacre from Nefertiti's dream. Aidan's blood was everywhere, and Nefertiti and Ur-Nammu were pinned down like grasshoppers in a field, trapped under the weight of a giant shadow. Setepenre was lancing Aidan open while Caelius sat back against a large stone, laughing, commanding her to continue.

Just seeing Setepenre's face threw my mind out of the battle. It was no wonder the Pharaoh had known Nefari had slept with me. Her teal eyes, lightly tanned skin, thick black hair, even the structure of her cheekbones . . . she was mine.

The awe quickly faded as she opened Aidan's gut, adding her laughter to Caelius's as she eyed him for approval.

Fury boiled to the surface. I had to kill him, to crush Caelius so Setepenre would never look at him like that again, like he was her *family*.

I called to Aidan. "The necklace works! Grab Setepenre so she doesn't try and take the hit!"

211

He nodded, spitting out blood as he wrapped his arms around her, his strength revealed. He'd been holding back, trying to get to Caelius without hurting her. Aidan and I shared a look; he knew she was my daughter.

She tore her teeth into his neck as he squeezed her tighter and ran toward the Zagros Mountains behind Gutium.

I quickly clasped the emerald stone around my neck. As Shea blasted her Light into the necklace, it shot fanged metal teeth into my sternum, clutching on to bone.

I staggered forward. It hadn't done that before. When Shea had kissed me outside the barn, that small spark from her Light had activated something, but this was different. With the metal from the stone's encasement growing deeper into my chest, I knew that this was going to work, or kill me in the process.

Caelius's eyes met mine, and his face twisted with pleasure. "I'm glad you're finally here, my son. I was getting bored having my Sete play with that puppy." He eyed Shea. "And you brought your bitch. Good. Now the real fun can begin."

I didn't respond. I used all the power I could summon, all that I had learned in Egypt with Moses. I called the essence of everything I had deep inside of me, shoving it into the emerald stone, feeding it power.

The necklace shot out an infused gray light—straight into Caelius's chest.

His flesh burned.

He howled in agony.

But I had no time to enjoy his pain. The necklace's power was sucking away my energy. As the blast bored into Caelius, its fiery power consuming his flesh, my body weakened further.

I fell to my knees. But it was not only me whose strength was being taken away as the blast continued. Shea joined me on the ground. Helena had been wrong; the necklace was *killing* us.

I tried to stop it, to rip off the necklace, but I couldn't. The metal—infused with whatever concoction Helena had devised, and combined with the powers of Shea and me—would finish what it started.

I choked.

The necklace was absorbing not just my body, but my will.

I looked at Shea. She looked weaker than I was. I reached for her. Our hands intertwined.

Was this how we were going to die? Side by side, giving our power over to kill the living incarnation of Darkness?

I prayed. If there was anything out there, if the Light cared about its small piece in Shea, I prayed that it would spare her. *Please*, I prayed, *let her break free.*

Caelius screamed one last time, then there was silence.

The necklace made a humming sound.

Then it fell from my chest, smoking. The bright green emerald had turned black.

I fell forward. Nefertiti, now free from Caelius's shadow form, ran and clutched me in her arms.

Ur-Nammu stepped over to hold Shea.

My voice was weak. "Is she okay?"

Nefari's eyes were firm. "Of course she is."

"I'm fine," Shea croaked out next to me. "I just feel like someone dropped a thousand-ton brick on my face."

"Is Caelius dead?" Nefertiti looked at Ur-Nammu, and he nodded. "There's nothing but a pile of ash."

His voice was filled with relief—as mine would have been too. After all of these years, after everything we'd been through, we'd *done* it.

I sat up and reached for Shea, pulling her into my arms. She rested her face on my chest. I leaned my head on hers.

We'd won.

Ur-Nammu stepped over to Nefertiti and held her. I caught a glimpse of her face as one small tear left the hardened mask. Then she broke, falling into her father's arms. They wept together. Thousands of years of slavery . . . finally at an end.

Tears welled in my eyes as well. Were we finally free? "Is it over?" I said aloud.

Now we could live. Paris could be every day. There was nothing to imprison our souls, nothing to chain us. And Shea was a Vessel. A Vessel could live as long as a vampire. We would have the ages to love each other.

I pulled back. "Where's Setepenre?"

Shea jerked up. "Where's Aidan?"

CHAPTER 13
SHEA

As if hearing me, Aidan was instantly by my side. The three of us held one another for a long time. Lucian and Aidan had an extensive and complicated past, but now there was nothing to keep them from being brothers again. My boys. It was nice to feel completely content, even just for a moment.

We pulled away when we heard Setepenre's scream as she raced to Caelius's ashes.

I felt heartless because I didn't care.

All I cared about was the fact that we were finally rid of Daddy Evil.

Setepenre was obviously one of Nefertiti's daughters from the looks of her, and apparently she was on Team Caelius. Then I saw her eyes . . .

Those perfect teal eyes.

I turned to Lucian, and his expression confirmed it: Setepenre was *his* and Nefertiti's daughter.

"I just found out today," Lucian confessed.

Okay, my perfect moment of contentment was now a little skewed. Still, honestly, even love child revelations couldn't shake my mood completely. I knew I should've been freaking out, but it made a weird kind of sense. Lucian and Nefertiti had a history. A long-ass history. And it didn't really surprise me that they had a child together.

Besides, I knew I could deal with my feelings later because right *now*, in *this* instant . . .

We were free.

Free!

If I felt this good, I could only imagine how Nefertiti felt. Sure, she'd have to deal with her psycho daughter, Setepenre, who was currently wailing like a banshee. And I was pretty sure she'd be looking for revenge. But Lucian and Nefertiti could probably pin her down long enough to wipe away the brainwashing that the master of evil had created. At least I hoped so for Lucian's sake.

I slowly stood up with Lucian. "We have to find where Caelius stashed my mother."

Aidan nodded and jumped to his feet. "I'll try to track her."

Setepenre finally came to her senses and whirled on Nefertiti. "How could you allow this? He was your father!"

Nefertiti's face was wracked with desperate concern. "My little Sete, Caelius was no one's father. He was a plague that needed to be stopped. Ur-Nammu is *my* only father, and *your* only grandfather. You will see, in time."

But Setepenre wasn't buying it. "Time cannot erase your betrayal! Grandfather was the only one who understood me, who loved me, who told me the truth and not your filthy lies! And now look what you've done! He's ashes. As if he never existed. Not even his true form survived!" she cried hysterically.

Not even his true form survived.

Chills raced down my spine. From everything I'd learned since this whole thing had started, Caelius was Darkness incarnate. Yes, we could destroy his flesh-made body because he had chosen to give up his shadow form to be human, but wouldn't that mean he would go back to being only Darkness again? Shouldn't we have seen some kind of crazy smoke monster or shadow creature or something, like we had when he'd been caged in his prison?

Maybe I was being paranoid, but that tiny seed of doubt was beginning to grow into an entire forest. I grabbed Lucian's arm. "Let's get out of here."

He reacted to the urgency in my voice. "What is it?"

"I just . . . I don't know . . . I don't want to jinx anything." I couldn't say what I was thinking. Maybe it was just an irrational fear.

Then we heard laughing.

A familiar, nails-on-chalkboard chuckle that made my whole being sink with dread.

I hated being right.

Nefertiti's gasp of disbelief and anguish made my heart squeeze for her—and for us.

This wasn't over.

Not by a long shot.

And we had nothing left to fight Caelius with.

Before us all, Caelius's body grew out of the ashes until he stood perfectly formed without a scratch on him.

Setepenre, still on her knees, grasped and held on to his leg in total adoration. Her tears were now tears of joy at seeing her "grandfather" in full health.

Caelius acknowledged her by placing his hand on her long black tresses and petting her like a dog. "My sweet Sete. You are the only child who stood by me, who is grateful for the life I've given you, the only one who is loyal to me and me alone."

Lucian placed his body in front of mine and was slowly backing us away from our worst nightmare. I could only imagine what was going on in his head, seeing his newly found daughter for the first time and watching as she lovingly stared at the creature he hated most in the world.

My brain could hardly take in what was happening. The sundial's power still surged through me, and it was making my mind fuzzy again.

I almost wanted to laugh out loud. This couldn't be happening. We'd defeated him. We'd killed him. Our powers united had finally destroyed the evil monster. And yet, the only thing that kept repeating in my head was the quote from Dark Helmet in the movie *Spaceballs*.

Evil will always triumph because good is dumb.

And then I *did* laugh. I couldn't control myself. Everything was so wrong that this whole situation struck me as absurdly funny.

Caelius appeared amused by my mirth. "I think your bitch has finally cracked, Lucian."

Lucian didn't respond. His body was rigid, battle ready, waiting for what his father was going to do next.

I stopped laughing. Things were starting to come into focus

again. If we were going to survive, we'd need to escape and go back to our life on the run. I needed to create a distraction.

Caelius milked the moment for all he could, knowing he had everyone's rapt attention. "My children"—he glanced at me and Aidan—"and *others*." He offered his hand to Setepenre, helping her to her feet. "I want to thank you from the bottom of my heart—"

I threw my hands forward, and a large beam of light engulfed his entire body. Setepenre was thrown back from the force, her skin burned from being so close.

Instead of screaming in pain, Caelius simply chuckled again, and with the snap of his fingers, my sundial-super-attack turned into a yellow, harmless mist, leaving only dust behind. Caelius brushed it away and looked at me with amused contempt. "Your Light doesn't work on me anymore, little Vessel." He pointed at Lucian and me. "You two made certain of that."

Nefertiti and Lucian exchanged puzzled glances, but I had the sinking feeling that I knew what was coming next. As in, refer back to the *Spaceballs* quote.

"We need to get out of here," I repeated. If super-juice couldn't affect Caelius, what could three vampires and an angel do?

"You're not going anywhere until I've crushed every cell in your body," Caelius said to me. I thought I would melt from his glare.

His threat sent Lucian into protective mode. He growled at his father and bared his teeth.

Caelius wasn't even remotely threatened, he simply looked more amused. "Did you think that I wouldn't know what your little gang was planning?" He looked at Nefertiti as her nails dug into Ur-Nammu's arms, her eyes wide with horror.

"Your pet, Helena, is a fascinating woman—and very inventive. You didn't think I would notice her little experiments? Well," he drawled, "I did. And, once I realized what she had in store for me, it wasn't difficult to tamper with her fragile mind and make her reverse that little device of hers."

Before we could absorb the truth of what he had just said, Caelius focused on me. "I needed to know what I was up against, of course, to know exactly how much power I'd be feeding on. I wanted to find out if it would be enough to bring me back to my full strength. I *let* you attack me before, with Gracuri. I lured you in with Lucian. I waited for you in that wet, dark cave, feeding him your parents. I didn't expect Lucian and Nefertiti to turn them, but that was icing. I pleaded for their help as you crushed my bones." He laughed again, making my skin crawl. "You never hurt me, Vessel. I was just gauging your power."

Caelius reached out to Lucian. Though he was yards away, the shadow of his hand brushed Lucian's cheek. "When you two used your joint powers with that necklace, you weren't killing me." He smiled viciously. "You were *restoring* me." He motioned with glee to the remnants that used to be his body. "Like a phoenix rising from the ashes. Tell me, Vessel, how does it feel to fail so completely to the Dark that you've even lost your *soul*? Do you all see how foolish you were to stand against me?" His shadow hand pulled back from Lucian and wrapped lovingly around Setepenre. "It matters not. I know who my true family is."

No soul?

He had taken my soul?

I still felt like I had a soul, but what would that really feel like anyway?

I had to push the thought aside so that I could survive this moment.

I couldn't believe we all just stood there, listening to his monologue. It was as if we were too shocked to believe that this was actually happening.

Setepenre bared her fangs at Lucian and Nefertiti in response.

It must have killed Lucian, seeing Setepenre's hatred of him, but he didn't show it. I knew he would spare her, but from the way he blocked me from Caelius, I also knew that he'd die protecting me.

This was it.

If we didn't run now, it would end with Caelius killing us all.

He was at full power.

Unstoppable.

Indestructible.

"Run!" Aidan screamed and launched himself at Caelius. He knocked Setepenre aside as if she were made of air, then began to speak a language I didn't recognize.

"No!" I shrieked.

Aidan was going to sacrifice himself to save us. He wasn't waiting for his brothers. He was going to die and transform himself, his soul, into Caelius's prison.

I didn't know if I had a soul or not, but I had to try and stop Aidan from killing himself. I threw my hands out to use all the power I had left in me. I connected to the ground, making the earth shudder and roll, trying to interrupt Aidan's chanting, but he continued.

His body started to glow.

I couldn't lose Aidan.

Not to Caelius.

I wouldn't let him die for me.

I brought out the wind, creating a hurricane of dirt and leaves, but it was as if Caelius and Aidan were in the eye of the storm, untouchable.

I had been so focused on my own terror, I hadn't noticed that Lucian had tried to rescue Aidan as well, but Setepenre stopped him. Her teeth sunk into his neck, and he was trying to pull her off without hurting her.

Then Aidan stopped his incantation and stood there looking as confused as I was.

Knowing that Aidan hadn't turned into super-prison-incarnate made me feel relieved. I immediately felt the drain of all the power I had been using. I dropped my connection to the elements; the air and ground went still.

Only Caelius seemed to know what was going on. He looked pleased with himself.

Again.

"You stupid beast. It's been over three thousand years! Aren't you wondering why your brothers haven't come to join you? It's because it was a onetime deal. Your prison won't work on me anymore! You failed your mission. I can't be killed or trapped. Your brothers will never leave the Light now, not even to save you." Caelius barely touched Aidan's chest, and his body went flying until it smashed into a boulder. I knew a fall like that wouldn't kill him, but seeing my best friend lying unconscious on the ground made me worried all the same.

Lucian managed to throw Setepenre off. She landed at Caelius's feet with a loud thud. I saw Lucian cringe at the impact.

I was growing weaker by the second. I wasn't sure how long I could stand.

This was it.

I was going to die.

All that time we'd spent on the run, planning, training, learning my powers . . . we were exactly where we'd started the first time we'd faced Caelius. Except now we didn't have Aidan's brothers to help.

I looked over at Nefertiti and Ur-Nammu.

They were with me.

All differences aside, we were together. If we were going to die, we'd die trying to hurt Caelius enough so some of us could escape.

I nodded to Nefertiti.

In this moment, we were soldiers bonded by our desire to take down our common enemy. She nodded back, respect gleaming in her eyes for the first time.

Here we go.

But before we could charge, six bodies raced onto the battlefield: Nefertiti's five daughters and my dad.

Normally, the last person I'd be afraid of was Jeff Harper. He was an architect for goodness sake! But seeing him with his fangs out gave me chills. I thought Dad grounding me for taking the car out when I was fifteen had been bad, but the way he looked now was terrifying.

I knew it wouldn't be enough to hurt Caelius, but maybe we could damage him so we could *all* run and survive.

We had to try.

Meky grabbed Aidan's still form and looked at her mother. "I have to save him."

Nefertiti gave Meky a nod of approval. "Go. And if none of us make it out, remember our Gutian oath. Let it live in you. Have the love that I cannot."

Tears streamed down Meky's face as she wrapped her arms around Aidan. They were gone in less than a second.

I felt immediate relief. Aidan would be safe. At least for now, anyway. Then it sunk in what Nefertiti had said. *Have the love that I cannot.* If I felt horrible, Lucian must have been feeling even worse.

"Oh, wonderful!" Caelius grinned. "The nonessentials have arrived. I was getting hungry."

My heart crushed from terror.

Daddy.

CHAPTER 14
LUCIAN

"**W**ait! Stop!" Why were they here? "You all have to run!" They had to leave!

"We are not leaving our family!" Jeff shouted as they all rushed Caelius, ignoring my pleas. He plowed through them effortlessly. My Sete was helping him, cutting her sisters open as they flooded in.

The ancient fear instilled by Caelius stirred in me, the belief that nothing I could do would be enough to keep those I loved alive. Caelius would win.

There was proof in his power now, in the destroyed amulet and our mass failure. But I was Gutian before I was *his*. I thought of my father on the battlefield, alone. And now, seeing this horde, my tribe—the people I loved—fighting the darkness that was Caelius, I would rather have died by their side than escape with Shea and live in the aftermath of their butchered bodies.

I closed my eyes.

The earth below my feet rumbled.

I called on the blood of every creature I could reach. Thousands of insects crawled from the ground and completely covered Caelius's new skin. He screamed. I made them form a shell around his limbs, entombing his body.

Setepenre howled, but I trapped her in the swarming insects at her feet, pinning her to the earth. I couldn't hurt her, not my daughter. I didn't care if she was loyal to Caelius. Even her screams as she tore at the insects scraped down the sides of my skull. *My Setepenre.*

"I will stay and fight, the rest of you leave!" I yelled.

They all shouted their protests as Shea stepped beside me and grabbed my hand. "We'll hurt him enough so that we can *all* escape together! We are weak, but we can do this; we can buy ourselves time!"

I couldn't give up hope yet. I still had to believe that love could win against Darkness. And if it couldn't, then I'd gladly bury my body here with my people and my heart in my homeland.

Caelius's cries turned to laughter as he reached out of the mass of insects.

Shea summoned the earth and lifted the ground, making it swallow Caelius, breaking every bone in his body.

He recovered quickly, bursting through the surface, his skin already fully healed despite being crushed. He reset his bones, his spine cracking with every vertebra as he stretched. He turned to me as he snapped his neck into place, his long form resembling a snake as he restored his concaved skull with the power he had derived from us.

Shea summoned the air, and I used it to carry my locusts.

The wind thrashed at his skin, tearing apart his reassembled bones while my insects crawled into every orifice, eating his insides.

Still Caelius laughed.

I knew it wasn't enough.

Was he growing stronger from our efforts?

I refused to accept my fears and dug deep. Yes, I was exhausted—the amulet had sapped all the reserves I'd had—but this was my *family* at stake. And if I was going to die here, I was going to make sure that Caelius remembered this place: Gutium, my home. I hoped this land would burn in his mind forever.

I closed my eyes. I drew strength from the surroundings, my true heritage. I pushed upon powers I had only suspected to exist. There was no time to doubt now, no time to question. What I suspected, what I hoped for, *had* to exist . . . or we were doomed.

The ground started shaking, but this time it wasn't Shea's power over the earth. Caelius looked at me with a new regard, like a proud father. I gazed at him in hate.

I called every mammal, every creature whose mind was easy to control. I had mastered insects, snakes, and a few other sea creatures, but this was different. I felt every heartbeat, every animal that had blood pumping in its veins, and I summoned it to our cause. I expanded my control, calling beasts from Gutium to Saudi Arabia. Their hooves and claws shook the dirt around us, the sky turning black with birds as they rushed toward our battle.

Shea pinned Caelius to the ground as the beasts attacked and devoured his flesh. She used the trees, shredding their limbs into stakes, shooting thousands of sharpened spears through his torn body, crushing his brain into the mud as large crows tore and dug out the pieces.

Setepenre began weeping again as her sisters and Jeff tore and ripped at what mush was left of Caelius. I joined them, using my bare hands as my power over the mammals faded along with the last bit of my strength.

"Everyone run, this should be enough!" I screamed.

Shea stood back, staggering. I reached, but she hit the ground before I could catch her.

"Shea!" I rushed over, knelt down, and held her still form to my chest. She had a heartbeat, but it was slow.

Something splattered on my neck. I held Shea close, one last time, and then set her gently on the grass. I touched the back of my hair: blood.

I didn't want to turn.

A gnarled claw dragged me to Caelius's feet. He laughed, lifting me from the ground into the air. He turned me around savagely. My mouth fell open, my eyes fixed on his visage. I'd seen this face on him before.

He flung Jeff toward Shea. Jeff's mangled body fell next to his daughter's.

Then Caelius held the rest of us suspended in the air with black claws that protruded from his stomach. His mouth oozing blood, his face twisted, he looked like the shadow creature from the caves. But it wasn't smoke this time, it was real—the monster that was inside Caelius piercing through his human flesh.

Spikes protruded out of his back like long, sharp hairs. His fangs were as large as his face. There were no whites in his eyes. They were red. Red and gushing blood.

I looked at all of the others' horrified faces. Even Setepenre was aghast at what her false "grandfather" had become, at what he *really* was.

I wasn't shocked or afraid. The only feeling burning in me now was anger. They hadn't escaped in time. I had to keep fighting for my family, for Shea.

I wanted to conjure the smoke, the shadow within myself, like I'd done in the cave. But, having devoured me, Caelius owned that part of me now, and conjuring it would make me his puppet. I cursed myself and my weakness. I was failing, and they all needed me now more than ever.

Caelius dragged Merytaten to his mouth, then ripped her open. Victorious, he snapped her in half and poured the blood of Nefertiti's oldest daughter over his face and mouth, lapping it up like the mutant beast he was.

"No! Stop!" I screamed, struggling to free myself from his grasp.

Everyone cried out, fighting against Caelius's claws. Nefertiti's voice was the loudest. He dropped Merytaten's body onto Setepenre. She screamed, reeling in disbelief. "Grandfather, no! You said you'd *punish* my sisters, but you wouldn't *kill* them! We're a family! We are *your* family!"

Something happened. His eyes cleared, the auburn color returning. Caelius scowled, lowering us to the ground. And then he spoke, his voice dark.

"Don't worry, Sete. You won't remember any of this. It was Shea who killed your sisters. You'll still be my little pet."

She hesitated, unable to fathom his betrayal.

Nefertiti called to her. "Leave, Setepenre! Save yourself!"

It took all of my strength, but I moved the insects that still had her pinned to the earth. Before Sete could run, Caelius flung her through the air. I lunged, but the barbs on his claws that were piercing through my torso grew deeper, cracking my rib cage in half. His grip was too tight, and I was weak.

He growled, pinning us all to the ground.

"Don't worry, Lucian. I just sent her to the place I'm keeping Molly. When my lovely Sete wakes up, she'll have new memories of this moment."

He reached for Ankhesenpaaten, her sweet brown eyes filled with terror. The Gutium words she'd spoken to me in Amarna sank to the pit of my stomach. *Though we fall, we will never fail because we have given ourselves over to glory.* Before I could plea, before I could move, he unhinged his jaws and swallowed her whole.

I cried out. "Stop! Stop, Caelius! *Please!* Setepenre was right! We are your *family!*"

Nefertiti begged. "Please, Caelius, I made a mistake! I'll never stand against you again! Just let them live! I'll serve you!"

Caelius only laughed in response, pulling Nefertiti's second youngest, Neferneferure, close. He brushed her hair, drinking her as he spoke to Nefari through the holes in her daughter's body. "It's not you that I want, dear Nefertiti. It never was. Besides, you had your chance. Our original deal was that if I saved Lucian, you and yours would be loyal to me.

"This is *your* doing, Nefertiti. I always keep my promises. If you had behaved, you wouldn't have to watch me eat your children." Neferneferure's eyes stayed on her mother, courageous until the last drop, when she shriveled into ash, drained to nothing under the power of Caelius's gaping, life-sucking mouth.

This was what I'd been afraid of. This was why I hadn't wanted them to come. Tears rolled down my face. I kept pounding my fists against his barbed claw around my waist. My knuckles were bloody, the bones crushed to mush, and still I couldn't loosen his grip. I tried to summon the beasts again, to do *something*. But the harder I struggled, the closer I came to blacking out like Shea.

"Spare them!" Ur-Nammu begged. "It was me! It was *my* idea to betray you, Caelius! I filled their minds with poison! I controlled them! Let them live! You can . . . you can *convince* them to stay. They'll be loyal! Kill me in their place!"

Seeing Ur-Nammu offer up his life, as if that was the only strategy left, broke me. And I knew it meant nothing to him; there was no quarter given by Caelius. No mercy.

I tried summoning anything alive that would listen, and still there was no response.

The power of Caelius was emanating in destructive circles, killing the grass, scorching the earth under our backs, and rendering me useless.

Caelius covered Ur-Nammu's mouth. "I tolerated you and the scratchy sound of your voice for all these years. Now, thanks to your disloyalty, I'll finally be rid of it. But there's an order to things. We can't just have chaos."

He stood us all up.

"The parents should always be the ones who watch their children die. I'll drink them first. Then your daughter, Nefertiti. You will be honored last, Ur-Nammu. I'll give you the pleasure of watching your child and all of your grandchildren cease to exist."

I closed my eyes. No, Caelius wasn't mentioning his ultimate triumph of torture; *I* would be last. All of this pageantry of death was to service his pleasure—and my pain.

Caelius had won.

He would always win.

I gritted my teeth as he laughed. He forced my eyes open with another one of his jagged claws. "Stay alert, Lucian. I need you to *see* what your life has cost. After Ur-Nammu, I'll drink your precious Shea, since her existence ruined my perfect Adam and Eve. Still, Nefertiti proved her unworthiness. But you, my boy, for you I still have *great* plans."

He shoved his claw deeper into my abdomen, crushing my spine, clenching down harder, holding me in a fist.

Blood poured from my mouth as I choked out, "Caelius, *please* spare them!"

"Your pleas means nothing to me now, boy." He wrapped his mouth around the fourth-born daughter, Sherit, whispering into her throat. "Your *whore* mother served her purpose, didn't she?" He shook her like a doll. She winced in pain but disappointed him with her silent acceptance of death.

His agitation shifted as he then stared at Nefertiti. The tears hadn't stopped falling from her eyes since Merytaten's death. The woman who rarely cried was now weeping uncontrollably. Caelius had destroyed her.

Feeding off of the fear and pain in Nefari's trembling limbs, Caelius's mood elevated as he continued. "Nefertiti did, after all, birth Lucian's baby, my beautiful Setepenre. She made a vampire with him as well: the Vessel's own mother. Two wonderful spawns of my favorite plaything. I think Nefertiti was Eve enough. And you, Sherit, like your sisters, were just a child of that meat sack

Akhenaten. You were always disposable. I never cared for you."
Tears streamed from Sherit's eyes as they closed. She mouthed to
Nefari, her voice a whisper, "Be strong, Mother. The flame that
is *our* people and what we stand for cannot be stamped out of
time . . ."

He licked the side of Sherit's face, a face I'd never see smile
again. Her features reflected the beauty of her grandmother, the
people from the Zagros Mountains—a people that no longer
existed.

Her words boiled inside me. Our Gutian code was dying,
along with its only living descendants, on the very soil of our
homeland. I thought about my mother, about Nefari, about
Aidan and Shea. Caelius was right—I would always lose what
I loved at the hands of those who were more powerful. I would
lose because I always fought for what I loved. Now I needed to
give up, to stand against the code of my people and let love go.

"You're right, Caelius," I growled. "You never cared for them."

He paused.

"You never cared for anyone . . . but me."

His grip on Sherit loosened. "Are you finally ready to play,
my boy?"

I nodded. "All this time, I never saw it. But now I do."

Caelius stepped toward me. He released his claw, retracting
it back toward his long frame. I stumbled forward, coughing as
the gaping holes from the barbs spilled blood down my chest,
soaking my pants. It didn't matter. Nothing mattered now but
this last sacrifice, this surrender.

I stepped toward him. He looked shocked and pleased as he
eyed Shea. "Her body must have given out now that it's soulless.

What will you do, boy?"

He wanted me to grab her and run, to leave the rest of them to die. I stood tall, imagining Onack's last moments on the battlefield, all of those spears stuck through his torso, the empty place by his side where I should have been. "Even this battle, you picked Gutium for *me*, didn't you?"

I felt his power lessen as his focus shifted to me alone.

I staggered closer, holding my open wounds. "I'm what you want."

He half smiled. "Is that so?"

"I'm all you've *ever* wanted, since you became flesh."

The smile left his face, and he was still. A sort of relief moved through his shoulders as his claws sagged. Finally, I was acknowledging his true desires.

I was also aware.

Aware that Aidan had returned, unnoticed by Caelius. He must have convinced Meky that he was going to fight. That or he'd lied to her, his love for Shea stronger than any bond.

I let a piece of my mind connect with his.

Aidan. I called to him beyond Caelius's focus. *I know why you came back. Get Shea and the others out of here.*

Aidan's voice was like the wind—soft, barely audible in my mind—as he protested. *I won't leave you, my brother. I will stay by your side and fight.*

But it was too late.

Caelius ran his fingertips through my hair, his large teeth receding, his face reforming into that of a flawless youth. Caelius's eyes filled with longing as his voice curved with a twisted sort of fondness. "Of course I handpicked this place. You may not remember, but this was the first time we met, not in Egypt. I have watched you your whole life. I never drank a human until I took you."

I swallowed hard. I couldn't fathom what his words meant, or how long he'd played a role in my life, how long he'd been watching me from afar.

I pleaded in my mind with Aidan one last time. *Please, brother, look around you! You'll have one chance. When I distract Caelius, get them all out of here.*

Seeing the mutilated bodies of most of Nefertiti's children, with Jeff and Shea passed out and Nefari and Ur-Nammu weeping, Aidan finally agreed.

Caelius chuckled. "I'm at full power now that I've drained the Vessel of her soul. If it pains you so much, out of kindness, I'll kill her first."

I prayed Caelius was wrong and Shea still had her soul. Either way, I knew what I had to do.

I placed my hand against Caelius's chest. He looked at it curiously, pleasure filling his gaze. It was the same look I'd seen in the caves when he'd bent me to his will, playing with his favorite toy.

"You are right, *Father*."

Now he smiled. A full grin. His grip on everyone was loose. He was barely holding on, his mouth salivating. "And so, boy, *this* is what it takes for you to finally call me Father."

"I was wrong, Father. All this time. I know now that I can't win. Not against you. I'll stop fighting. Now . . . now that I know it has been *you* all along." I knew what I had to say, what his ego and empty heart wanted to hear. I pushed further. "I didn't realize, but I see it now. It is you whom I've wanted, you whom I *need.* You're the only one who really cares about me. Look at all you've done to prove it. After all of this time, you're my *God,* aren't you, Caelius?"

Caelius lunged forward and kissed me, claws and spikes disappearing into his chest as he dropped the others like useless sandbags. I kissed him back, hard, pulling him deeper into the embrace. He wrapped his body effortlessly around mine and lifted us into the air.

The others were gone in an instant. They'd escaped. Aidan had saved them.

Caelius didn't care. He was busy with me, tearing my clothes off, sinking his teeth into my neck. For once, I didn't resist. I needed to give them time. He moaned with ecstasy.

"You're all I've ever wanted," Caelius whispered into my ear as his hips shoved against mine.

"I know." I practically gasped the words. Caelius mistook it for passion, believing that the fire I felt was for him. Yes, there was fire, a gasping from the effort. It was all I could do to stop the spark within me from fighting him off.

The others needed to hide themselves. And to buy that time, here in Gutium I was offering up my life and my pride, as I should have done all those centuries ago on the battlefield next to my family.

I peeled off his clothes.

Our bodies pressed against each other, naked under the light of a full moon.

"I surrender everything. I will serve only you."

When he learns how I've betrayed him, I hope that my death is at least enough to buy them the chance to live.

I whispered into his ear, "I am yours now, Caelius, body and soul."

EPILOGUE
MOLLY

I waited patiently for Grandfather. He'd said he had to punish his misbehaving children (my parents) and then he would be back. That statement alone was the reason I'd never had kids. It made my skin crawl just thinking about how that Vessel had called me "mother." How dare she? As a human I had never even considered having a child, and for her to speak such a lie in front of my new parents and Grandfather? It was humiliating.

Still.

There was something so familiar about her.

I pushed the thought from my head like Caelius had shown me. It was quite easy now. Anytime a stressful thought crept into my mind, I would visually swat it away like a fly. It was empowering.

I wished I had possessed that skill as a human. My depression had been so strong, I'd been ready to die. When Grandfather had tried to compel me to feed Lucian with my blood, I'd hesitated at first, but then he'd whispered in my ear that I'd find peace. It was as if the Universe had finally given me my wish and was letting me end it all.

When I'd awoken as a vampire, I'd been crushed. All I'd wanted was the peacefulness of death that Grandfather had promised.

But I loved my life now. Draining mortals made me feel powerful, as if I could do anything. I'd never felt that way as a human. Back then I'd been weak, tired, and miserable. Jeff had been my only light, but I'd kept him in the dark for so long that I didn't know if he still wanted me. I missed him terribly, but Grandfather had said I might not see Jeff again and that killing him may have to be one of the punishments for my parents.

I didn't see how killing my husband would mean anything to Mother and Father, but Grandfather seemed to think Father would be hurt the most by this because of his feelings for the Vessel. Why did she care about me or Jeff anyway? She must really believe we were her parents. She had been so convinced. So sure.

I pushed the thought away. I couldn't even remember her name. Grandfather had said it wasn't important, since he was going to kill her anyway, and that I should just refer to her as the Vessel.

My heart surged when thinking of Grandfather. He was so good to me, and I wanted to show him how much I loved him. He'd given me a mission to find Father's last two Second-Borns, and I wasn't going to fail him. So as soon as Grandfather left, I used my amazing new sense of smell and found them almost instantly. Soaring across the skies was the most exhilarating sensation—I was so fast!

I had captured and brought both of Father's Second-Borns to my hiding place in less than an hour. I couldn't wait for Grandfather to return and see that I'd succeeded.

The only problem was that they smelled so good. I wanted to pop their heads off and drink them myself. I pushed the thought from my brain and sat, comfortably waiting for Grandfather to arrive. I just wished he'd hurry.

I was *really* hungry.

Other Books by Hina McCord

Ivory

Love & Dark Series (with Becca C. Smith):
Vessel
First Born
Gutian Code

Other Books by Becca C. Smith

The Riser Saga:
Riser
Reaper
Ripper

The Atlas Series:
Atlas
Grigori Returned
The Underworld

Alexis Tappendorf Series:
Alexis Tappendorf and the Search for Beale's Treasure
Alexis Tappendorf and the Search for Atlantis

The Dream Diaries:
The Dream Diaries
The Dream Diaries: Blood Ties

Love & Dark Series (with Hina McCord):
Vessel
First Born
Gutian Code

SHEA Chapters Written by:
Becca C. Smith

Becca fell in love with storytelling at an early age. The first book she read was The Lion, The Witch and The Wardrobe and she's been looking for the door to Narnia ever since! Becca is a passionate reader, consuming anything sci-fi or fantasy. Mix it in with YA and she is a fan for life. So it's no surprise that she writes in these genres as well. When Becca isn't writing, she loves to sew. From Mortal Instruments rune pillows, to elaborate Firefly/Serenity bags, Becca loves to create!

LUCIAN Chapters Written by:
Hina McCord

Hina McCord is a novelist, A.K.A. an avid bullshitter; that's why she lives in L.A.. She's been writing for as long as her ancient mind can remember, devouring tales like an anemic vampire roaming the streets in hot pink heels, always thirsty for more. When she's not writing, she's making steampunk weapons, sewing giant plant-eater Mario plushes, making costumes for some film bloke or cosplayer, and sculpting/casting movie prop replicas while gardening in her urban apartment. Her favorite tools? A soldering iron, a blowtorch, a band saw, a sonic screwdriver, a replicator and an active imagination.

www.ingramcontent.com/pod-product-compliance
Lightning Source LLC
Chambersburg PA
CBHW020637260626
47157CB00008B/2793